Mrs Rickaby's Lullaby

Julie Thorndyke

Mrs Rickaby's Lullaby

Mrs Rickaby's Lullaby
ISBN 978 1 76041 709 3
Copyright © Julie Thorndyke 2019
Cover image: *Dendrobium phelongrium*, Adam Forster,
1848–1928, National Library of Australia, nla.obj-135418922

First published 2019 by
GINNINDERRA PRESS
PO Box 3461 Port Adelaide 5015
www.ginninderrapress.com.au

Contents

1

Nocturne

Missy is perched on the wide top of the wing-backed chair before the window: curtains are drawn for night time, and the glow of a single lamp glosses the dense silkiness of her white coat, illuminates the pale blue irises of her almond eyes as she endows me with a confident, unblinking look, as only cats can.

She rolls into a more comfortable position and settles, as I fall into a rhythm, typing words as one might practise scales up and down, melodic quadruple octaves travelling the keyboard in that hypnotic fashion that lulls the mind and opens the metaphysical heart.

The night is chilly, a mid-autumn night, quiet and full of repose. I cannot hear any possums or flying foxes outside; these soft night creatures may go about their business unnoticed. There is no traffic noise, no parties in the neighbours' backyards, no sirens on the distant highway. It is just me, the cat and the keyboard, keeping our date with our elusive friend, and hoping she will turn up.

It's not as easy as you would think to get the words on the page, even with conditions so near perfect as they are right now, in my cosy room. Shall I pull out my pile of hastily scratched notes, gathered in spare minutes in shopping centres, doctors' waiting rooms and public spaces? Will they amount to anything that will grow and flourish, blossom and bear fruit, or are they simply worthless seeds that will be cast away into the furnace? (Hang on a minute; this is getting a little melodramatic. We aren't that kind of writer, are we? The cat stirs and blinks. Let's get into something a little less apocalyptic.) This is only an article for the *Orchid Society Journal*, I tell myself. Nothing Missy and I can't handle. I'm not a writer, really – well, I have published a book or too, but actually I am a botanical illustrator, and the words are subservient to the pictures. Words never come as easily to me as the curve of a leaf in sharp B pencil, or the flow of watercolour on a crimson petal. But I do my best, and usually it is enough.

The window is illuminated by the flash of a car headlight. Missy does her stand-and-stretch-into-an-S-shape manoeuvre, which is so appealing in a kitten. There is the sound of people laughing, voices whose words I cannot make out, the slam of a car door. Footsteps.

I leave my place at the desk and go to the window for a peek. It is my neighbour, Irene, who lives across the narrow street in our retirement community. She is not alone – a dark-suited man is following her onto the porch, carrying her suitcase (she has been away travelling for two months), chatting at the door. When he pecks her cheek and turns back to the BMW in the driveway, I am relieved. I have better things to do than worry all night about Irene and a dark-haired stranger she has picked up somewhere on her travels. Hang on a minute – does she have a brother? No. No family at all that she will admit to. No doubt I'll hear all about it in a day or so: Irene and I aren't close, but of all the women in the village (and we are mostly women here) we are the two with most in common, the most simpatico, as they say. We rely on each other for conversation, and to look after each other's orchids when either of us is away.

Irene and I met at the Orchid Society. Her interest is mainly in the small, rare species; I like cymbidiums, rock orchids, anything really, that I can get to grow. Anything I can paint. My courtyard is full of plants, in various stages of development. Irene is more selective and gives away many of her plants. Indeed, she gave me most of the ones that line my little oasis. She is an expert at propagation. Irene was a skilled surgeon, and even now works for Doctors Without Borders in various developing countries, doing what she can for children in need. She really is an admirable person, travels not merely for pleasure, but to 'make a difference' as the cliché goes, as well as see foreign places and experience other cultures. Not the champagne flutes and cruise ships for her, oh no. Perhaps that unknown man was another doctor? He certainly had the assured bearing of a cultured man. Well, perhaps I'll hear about that tomorrow. The cat should go out and I should go to bed: this article for the *Orchid Society Journal* will have to wait for tomorrow. When the yawns begin, at my age you have to obey the sandman and go to bed promptly, otherwise you'll miss that night train and be awake, fretting, all the midnight hours.

The shower is hot and steamy, but I don't stay in too long. Just enough to warm myself, relax tight neck muscles that have been hunched over the computer keyboard. I turn on the classical radio station, which always plays the right sort of pleasant bedtime sounds, Mozart or Brahms; slip into my pretty aqua nightgown, gift from my daughter Susan in Madrid. It pleases me to handle the fluffy bedsocks she sent with it for my last birthday; I give my seventy-one-year-old feet a rub with arthritis cream before slipping on the socks. My son Mike, in Beijing, phoned for my birthday. He is never organised enough to send presents.

Both are single: I can't think why they want to travel the world instead of settling down. Certainly doesn't come from me, and Howard, bless him, was never one for travelling either. Although he loved to jog every morning and was one of those men who could never quite sit still. I blow a kiss to his photograph on the bedroom wall. My double bed seems little in this room that Howard never shared, but it is already warm with my electric blanket, the doona soft and comforting.

My little villa is quiet, and there is no sound from outside. My bedroom is at the front of the house. There is another bedroom at the back, which is actually larger, but is well lit and more suitable for my painting gear. I have a single bed in there for visitors, squeezed in beside my easel; but it gets more use as a storage place for unfinished pictures. I do more painting in the living room – the dining table always has an unfinished picture set out with brushes and pigments. I find that it is easy to be busy when unwanted neighbours drop in, if the evidence is before their eyes. I still do commissions for books and journals, apart from the Orchid Society, but I take my time over them, pick and choose.

Missy trips in on her soft cat feet, right on cue, and finds a comfortable space at the end of the bed. I read a chapter of my current library book; nothing too exciting, just the measured sentences of a certain Scottish author who will lull me into rest. At eleven precisely, I switch off the radio and the light. Missy is purring.

*

There are times when I wish for a larger front garden. More than the narrow, pebble and mondo grass border that separates me from the road. A sound buffer of wide lawn and dense shrubbery. This is one of those times. The bedside clock reads 11.45 p.m. and Missy is rubbing her sweet kitten nose on my cheek. Outside, car doors are opening and shutting, a car motor is revving and there is muffled laughter. I don't have to leave my bed to twitch the curtain just a little to see who is making the racket. It is the same car back again, in Irene's drive. I can see the BMW logo clear as day. This time the man – I am sure it is the same one – is casually dressed, but just as attentive. He opens the car door for Irene, who gets in, trapping her long, ethnic scarf in the door, and so the door must be opened and shut again, there is more laughter, and finally the man drives the car away, not before illuminating my Missy's white whiskers with a flash of headlights, and causing her to take a leap for the windowsill. She knocks down a tiny china vase. Fearing she has cut her paws, I get out of my cosy bed and investigate. I sweep up the fragments of porcelain, set them aside on the kitchen bench. Missy is unhurt. I make warm milk in an effort to regain my sleep wave and go back to bed with my Scottish author. I read until 3 a.m.

*

'Eileen? Eileen Rickaby? Are you there?' It is Irene calling at the front door.

I've spent the morning deadheading the orchids in my sun-filled rear courtyard. Missy is helping, rubbing her sleek body against my calves, hoping for a treat. For three days I have kept an eye out for Irene, keeping the best coffee mugs handy and a supply of her favourite gluten-free almond slice in the tin ready for when she will call. I take my time in answering.

At the door, Irene gives me an enthusiastic hug and a cheek kiss.

'Have you been jet-lagged?' I ask.

'Not a bit,' laughs Irene. 'But it has been a bit of a whirl the last few days. Here…' she thrusts a package into my hands. 'I think you'll enjoy this.'

I unwrap the brown paper to find a plastic box, the size of a takeaway food container. I lift the lid to find a small plant nested in moss. The delicate foliage of the tiny plant, and the textures of the moss, make my fingers itch for a drawing pencil.

'A Cambodian orchid,' explains Irene.

'But how did you get it through customs?' I place the present carefully on the dining table beside my brushes and paints.

'Well…Ralph was bringing in a refrigerated carry bag of tissue samples for testing…there was plenty of room.'

'Ralph? The owner of the BMW?'

Irene actually blushes. 'You've been watching, then.'

I defend myself on the grounds of sleep-deprivation. 'I really couldn't help hearing you,' I said. 'Behaving like a couple of teenagers in the middle of the night.'

'Ralph isn't a quiet man,' she admits.

'A doctor?'

'Heavens, no, he is a medical administrator – a numbers man. Setting up hospitals, quality control, logistics, that sort of thing.' She grins. 'Lots of fun, having a man court you after all this time.'

'Are you lovers, then?' I ask.

'Noooo, but…'

'I see.'

Irene has never married; work has been the focus of her life. There had been affairs, but not lasting relationships. The men she had loved usually opted for marriage and family with someone else, in the long-term. She isn't bitter about this, knowing that her choice of life and career is hers alone. It is strange to see her so excited about a man.

'I think it would do best in a little terrarium,' says Irene, examining the little orchid. 'You know, like the glass-domed ones in the gift shop in town. Why don't we go and get one today? Have some lunch out?'

'You're on,' I reply. 'But what about Ralph?'

'He's busy,' says Irene. 'Driven up to Byron Bay on business. But he's coming back on the weekend to stay.'

'Irene, you don't have a spare room,' I jibe.

Her pointy elbow lands in my ribs.

'Oow,' I complain. 'He looks…young.'

'Sixty-five,' she replies. 'What's ten years?'

Irene doesn't look her seventy-five years, I grant her that. I sigh. 'I bet he's married.'

'Widowed,' says Irene. 'Twice, poor man.'

*

Terrarium bought, we settle down to a proper catch-up over cappuccinos and toasted sandwiches. Irene tells me about her trip: the hiking she had done, a little sightseeing before two weeks work at a children's hospital in Cambodia. How Ralph had worked with her to obtain the necessary medical supplies; how he had driven her to outlying villages in his jeep, so that outpatient clinics could operate.

'He does a great deal of good,' Irene says. 'Fundraising and so on. He puts in quite a lot of his own money, too. Pays for his own travel expenses.'

'Well-off, then?' I query. 'Unusual for a public servant.'

'Made some good investments, I think. No one to spend his money on. There should be more philanthropists in this country.' Irene has strict views on this subject. Her own estate is to be divided among her favourite charities when the time comes.

'I think we will need more sphagnum moss,' she says. 'Better stop at the nursery on the way home.'

It was a full day of Irene's company: at home we potted up the orchid in the terrarium, watered it and placed the glass dome over the plant. I put it on the dining table, where I could keep an eye on it, and sketch it, as much as I liked.

'It should thrive there,' says Irene. 'Listening to your day-long bloody Mozart.'

'An ideal subject for the next issue of the *Orchid Society Journal*,' I reply. 'Although I think we should omit the details of its dubious origins.'

'Keep that cat away from it!' she warns.

Missy is eyeing the new item on the table with interest.

'I don't allow her on the table,' I protest, opening a bottle of wine.

But we both know that more than once the cat has upset my painting equipment and ruined half-finished illustrations with her curiosity.

Irene edits the article I have just finished, making a few suggestions, correcting details, admiring the drawings. 'We are science and art,' she says. 'A perfect partnership.'

'I'll drink to that,' I agree, pouring another glass of wine.

Irene leaves about 7 p.m., after nibbling for an hour on cheese, vegetable croutons and hummus, and finishing a bottle of Semillon. I do a little drawing, although the light is not ideal, and go to bed early. I sleep soundly with no interruptions.

The next few days flow along peaceably. There's an *Orchid Society Journal* committee meeting (Irene sends an apology). I clear my pantry of expired food items, go to my t'ai chi class, take Missy to the vet for her vaccination. I don't see much of Irene, apart from a distant wave or a brief chat as I stroll around the village, collecting autumn leaves to sketch for a magazine cover commission I have just accepted.

Mostly, I draw and paint my new orchid. I take a reference photograph every day, to record the growth. I am engaged in a quest to render the reflections of light on the glass dome in watercolour; to capture the dense textures of moss. Small buds are swelling on the orchid plant – daily I check their progress. I do not know what colour the blooms will be. I decide to research the orchid on the computer. Hours later, frustrated by my slow progress (my son says I need a faster modem), there is nothing for it but a visit to our local library, which is also a branch of a regional university library, well-stocked with botanical information, thanks to the local Orchid Society.

'Rickaby. R.I.C.K.A.B.Y.' I make myself smile, laboriously spelling my surname for the child working at the library service counter. What can he be, fourteen years old? On work experience? I read his name tag and spell mine again, more slowly. He can't truly be permanent staff?

'Yes, there you are!' He gleams with pride at his achievement. 'I knew you would be on the database somewhere.' He scans the orchid books I want to borrow, admires the pictures on the cover. 'I have a nice dendrobium myself,' he offers. 'You mustn't over-water them, though.'

Smiling as graciously as I can, I leave the library precinct, which seems to be more devoted to computers than books. Still, the visit has served my purpose, and I have lots of information about Cambodian orchids saved to my USB drive, the books I have borrowed, and other, more potentially startling, pieces of unexpected information. I've been surfing the net, as they say, and checked out the Doctors Without Borders website. I admired the blog Irene had written about her trip to Cambodia, peered at the pictures of her and Ralph beside a waterfall. (Pictures never load up well on my home computer – as Mike says, the modem is too slow.) Ralph's black hair was dark and slick as if wet from swimming; Irene's sarong also looked damp, and her hair wet and dishevelled. His name was in blue, indicating a hyperlink (I am not as computer illiterate as my son thinks) so I clicked and followed it, reading and learning quite a lot about Mr Ralph Furnace as I traversed the web. It only took a little cut and paste Googling to find out even more; wedding pictures from both his marriages, sad messages of remembrance on the funeral parlours' websites for both his unfortunate late wives. So sad, to lose two beloved spouses in the space of four years! Some of the relatives were very free with their grief-filled comments on Facebook (don't they know how to keep their information private?) Sudden death does happen, no doubt about it, but to have two women both die within a year of marrying the same man, causes unknown, is ground for concern.

All the way home, I worry about Irene, knowing how smitten she is with Ralph. How can I possibly protect her from this man? Get a grip, Eileen, I tell myself. Irene is capable of looking after herself. She won't rush into any relationship without being sure. I can't tell her I have been snooping on Facebook about Ralph behind her back, can I?

Key in the lock, I find a little handwritten note pushed under my front door. *Gone away for a week or so*, it read. *Spending some time up north with Ralph's family. Will you water my orchids please? Thanks, Irene.*

Which family? The stepdaughter and grandchildren from the second marriage or the first wife's brother in Queensland? I must be careful what I say when she gets back. Too easy to let a detail slip out and reveal my covert research.

In bed that night, I say a little prayer for Irene while I listen to Mozart and Missy circles around, to find a comfortable spot. Keep my dear friend safe, I ask. Let her see Ralph for the snake he is.

Sleep doesn't come for a long time, despite the deep silence enveloping the neighbourhood.

2

Divertimento

Two days later, I decide to check Irene's orchids. Opening my china cabinet, I take her spare house key from my mother's Spode sugar bowl. I never take sugar. If visitors want to sweeten their tea, I direct them to the small canister in the pantry. My mother's Spode has long been retired. Irene has a key to my villa, as well – I am not sure where she keeps it. It is a fine afternoon, but I wrap myself in a light jacket before going out, and pop my digital camera in the pocket, thinking to take a walk afterwards, perhaps to the man-made lake by the golf course, and scout for more autumn foliage vistas to paint.

After letting myself into Irene's place, I take a few minutes to check each room, make sure everything is as it should be. There have been few break-ins in our retirement village in the past, but you never know. The lounge looks as it should, Irene's Asian sculptures and few really good paintings in place, a scarlet throw draped over the arm of her leather couch. The bathroom window is locked, but one of the taps is dripping, so I turn it more firmly off to stop the flow. A man's razor and shaving cream are on the vanity – Ralph must be growing bristly by now or have a spare set. Oh well, some women find that sexy, the tabloids say. The bedroom windows are also secure, but a velour robe has fallen to the floor. As I pick it up to rehang it on the hook behind the door, a strong whiff of aftershave assaults my nostrils. A cheap scent, not a refined brand, such as Howard used.

All in all, it is a relief to open the sliding door to the courtyard and breathe fresh air. I find a little watering can, and go into the kitchen to fill it. There is another odour there. Milk that has gone off? I open the fridge to check. No milk, just some sealed containers and a six-pack of lager. I hadn't picked him for a beer drinker. Looking elsewhere for the smell, I open a door that conceals the kitchen tidy. Yes…that's it. Fish scraps, leftover chips, prawn tails, oyster shells. The remains of a seafood platter that hasn't been properly thrown away. I take out the full bin liner and tie it firmly, then encase it in another layer of plastic. I take it and an empty bottle of Moët straight to the outside bin.

Back inside, hands cleansed and air freshener sprayed, I am finally able to water the orchids. These are just a little on the dry side. One of the dendrobiums is looking wonderful, with cascades of white blooms. I decide to photograph it for the orchid journal, knowing Irene will be flattered. The sky is dark with storm clouds now, so I won't have time for a walk after all. I take several shots of the orchid, from various angles, lock up carefully and return home.

I grill a bit of salmon and boil some new potatoes. A few spears of asparagus complete my meal. Missy is hovering for her share of the fish, and I am generous, too liberal perhaps, on account of the Chablis I have opened on a whim. I don't get around to painting, but take a hot bubble bath instead, as the thunder cracks overhead and flashes of lightning make Missy's tail expand and her neck ruff fill out like a frill-necked lizard. Storms have never bothered me – in fact, I forgo Mozart and the Scottish author altogether and fall directly asleep at 10 p.m.

*

A Sunday afternoon in early winter; not cold, no wind, just gentle sunshine to warm but not burn the skin. I take the opportunity of a vitamin D nap on the wicker sun lounge in my orchid-lined courtyard. Missy discovers my intention and trots over, leaping onto the lounge and curling up next to my toes.

Head supported by a down cushion in the colourful Flemish tapestry cover Susan sent for Mother's Day, I doze and dream, my mind releasing images of Susan and Mike as babies, toddling on beaches, making sandcastles, being carried on the sturdy tanned shoulders of their father, as I swim in shallow lagoons or dive into foaming waves. How relieved the children had always been when I re-emerged from the ocean, despite their father's reassurance and diversions. They didn't know I was quite safe in that gentle sea; that I had been a champion long-distance swimmer in my teens. Howard knew, of course; but we didn't speak of it. It was too bound up with tragedy to be a topic I ever wanted to discuss.

My dreams change, roll back to those days of cold, early morning swims and training in all weathers; the monotony of miles of open sea water, the mind games you invented to trick yourself to carry on and reach your goal. The taste of salt is in my mouth, my fingertips wrinkled and sticky with brine…

I wake, Missy too, abruptly alert and standing with her tail straight up as the side gate creaks open and a shopping trolley is wheeled into my courtyard.

'Hullooo! Caught you napping!' says Annette, secretary of the Orchid Society and general village busybody.

I am annoyed: Annette is one of those hyperactive joiners, who can't sit still for a second, and believes that her main reason for existence is to shake everyone else out of their hard-won tranquillity and keep them busy too. Orchid Society, Art Society, Book Club; Garden Club, Craft Group, University of the Third Age; Church Choir, Society for the Prevention of Cruelty to Animals…she is a member of all these groups, and always has ideas for more. Annette is one of the reasons I keep my painting gear in full view on the dining room table – I can point to my paid employment and claim to be far too occupied to join another one of Annette's groups or causes.

Missy hisses and jumps off the lounge, darts to the cat flap and disappears into the house. I wish I could follow, but I am the mouse in the trap.

'I can't sleep in the day myself,' Annette says in her sing-song voice. 'Keeps me awake all night, if I do.' It is a well known fact that she locks her door at 6 p.m. every night and does not appear again until she goes for her morning walk at 6 a.m. next morning.

'Fortunately, I'm not so tied to routine,' I lie. 'But I have been working day and night to finish a commission, so have earned my rest.' This is true: I have been working hard to finish the autumn leaf cover and illustrations, for tomorrow's deadline.

'Oooh, how interesting! It must be wonderful to be so creative,' she coos. 'I'd love to see it,' she hints.

'Sorry, all packed up for the courier,' I say firmly, thankfully, not wanting to have the inevitable comments from Annette about it being too late for an autumn cover and having to explain about the forward planning that must necessarily occur in the publishing industry.

'Oh well, you must show me the next project. Really, I love all your work. The illustrations in this issue of the *Orchid Society Journal* are just lovely.' She hands me a bundle of the freshly printed journals. 'I just dropped by to give you these. Irene's copies are there too,' she added. 'She is still away, isn't she? Will you pass them on?'

'Yes. Yes, of course,' I reply, thankful for this simple reason for the visit, hoping there is no sting in the tail. 'I must go over and water her plants later on.'

'You're watering her plants today?' Annette asks. 'Doing your normal walk? Would you mind taking the journals to members on this side of the village? I've done the other side and the mail-out, and with my hip playing up I think I've done enough walking today.'

Of course I must agree, noticing that the pile of journals is larger than it should have been for just Irene and me.

'Nice cushion!' says, Annette, picking up the gift from my daughter, looking closely at the fabric.

'Susan sent it,' I say.

'She's an artist too, isn't she?'

'Art restorer, historian,' I reply.

'You think I don't understand about mother love,' says Annette suddenly. 'Being a spinster. But…I had a child. I was sixteen. The nuns adopted it out. Never saw him again. Somewhere out there, I hope my boy is alive and happy. Not a day goes by that I don't think of him.'

'Oh, Annette…' I do not know what to say.

'I keep busy,' says Annette. 'Keeping busy is the only way.'

The phone rings, and Annette leaves, mission accomplished. I go inside to answer.

It is Irene. 'We will be home on Sunday!' she chants. 'And we have NEWS!'

Uneasy, I still manage to keep a cheerful voice in our brief conversation, assure her everything at home is fine. I must hurry now to water the plants and deliver all those blasted journals.

I'm getting the key from the china cabinet when the phone rings again.

'Mum!' Mike shouts. 'Mum, I'm coming to Sydney!'

'How lovely! No need to shout. When?'

'Next week. For a conference. I'll drive up and see you on the weekend, OK? Just a flying visit. Be there Saturday night. Love you. See you soon.'

Always in a rush, always impulsive, Mike is my only son and I love him to pieces.

My mind is in a whirl. I walk around the village, delivering journals, chatting to the people I encounter. I stop for a cup of tea with my friends Larry and Joan, but mostly I put the journals into letter boxes. It would take far too long to call on everyone who belongs to the society.

At last I turn the bend back to my own street and stop at Irene's place. The house is in order; the orchids need just a little water. The dendrobium I have photographed before is looking wonderful – the petals have changed colour now and I must capture the new tones. I don't have my camera with me, so I take the orchid home to observe. I will only keep the plant a day or so.

In the following days, I busy myself cleaning the house and shopping for food Mike will like. My mind is full of plans and lists. I forget all about returning Irene's dendrobium. I'm up late and busy on Friday, until finally at midnight Missy indicates, with a meow at the bedroom door, that it really is time to turn in. Too excited to sleep, I lie awake until dawn, only then falling asleep to wake feeling head-achy and cross. Not a good start to the day when I've so much to do.

After taking some paracetamol, I open the tub of local honey I purchased at a farmer's market. Mike always loved honey as a child. Perhaps he still does – I have no idea. I plunge the knife deep into the tub and bring up a thick, generous dollop. It is luscious and aromatic, gorgeous on the hot toast. I sip my English breakfast tea as Missy circles my chair, hoping for a treat. I add cat food to the list I am checking and ticking off as I eat. I make another piece of toast and honey to fortify me. Missy leaps up and licks a droplet of honey I have spilled on the bench. I should swat her away – I don't approve of cats on tables and kitchen benches – but today I let her have this bit of sticky pleasure. Once it is licked up, I stoke her head gently and lift her down to the floor. Purring, she goes to the French window, looks out, and begins washing her face in a determined, businesslike fashion.

Taking my cue from the cat, I bustle around sanitising the kitchen bench, washing my cup and plate, putting away the last of yesterday's shopping, emptying the kitchen tidy. At the rubbish bin at the front of my house, I greet two gents walking with their golf carts, off to the course for a friendly game. There is a gardener mowing the verge with a ride-on mower, wafting the smell of damp, cut grass into the air. A willy wagtail is dancing on the brick pillar next to my driveway. I pause for a moment and sketch it in my mind. I always find drawing birds a challenge – how to render a sense of movement, and not have them turn out static and lifeless, like stuffed specimens in a glass museum case. If I didn't have so much to do, I would have a try at a wagtail this morning – but, no. Must focus on the task at hand.

In the spare room, I have already cleared the bed and made it up with clean sheets, but there is a great deal of clutter, and ideally I would like to put away my painting stuff from the dining table so Mike and I can eat there. This room has a generous, built-in wardrobe which unfortunately is already stuffed with things that have no other place to be.

Now let me tell you, quite firmly in my own defence, that when downsizing to this little villa, I did a great deal of culling, sorting and throwing away. In this wardrobe I have a very small fraction of the stuff that had accumulated over forty-five years of marriage to Howard. There are two large plastic tubs, one marked Susie and the other marked Mike: these hold the school photographs, trophies, precious finger-painted Mother's Day presents and hand-sewn felt bookmarks that I could never throw away. There is another smaller tub labelled Howard, in which I keep my husband's birth and death certificates, the letters he sent to me in our courtship, and a few sentimental items of clothing that, when pressed against my cheek, provide a little sense of his presence.

The fourth tub isn't labelled; it seems silly to put one's own name on a box of memorabilia. In this tub there are scrapbooks crammed with newspaper cuttings, also ribbons and medals from my long-distance swimming career. Oh yes, I was once a champion! Won race after race, coached by my father. It all came to an abrupt end when my parents were killed in a car crash, driving across the country to a race; I was in the back seat, but unharmed. A nineteen-year-old suddenly alone in the world, I fell into a deep depression, also suffered a severe case of glandular fever. I pull out a photo of my mum and dad, standing in front of the old Holden. The few photographs I have of them are in the box, too – for some reason I have never put many photos around the house as some retired people do. I slide my parents back into the box, secure the lid tight.

Beside the tub are a few large acrylic canvases I painted in my early widowhood – not particularly good, any of them, but representing a phase of my life too recent to be thrown away. A large plastic bag of winter clothes I have not needed in this climate, and not worn for years. They can go to the op shop! Various other cardboard boxes, mostly empty – these I can toss.

I take the largest box to the dining table and stow away my brushes and palettes, sketching block and sponges. All that is left on the dining table are two orchids: the one from Cambodia, doing well in the terrarium, and Irene's dendrobium in full bloom. These I slide to one end: Mike and I can eat at the other.

I close the wardrobe in the spare room with a sense of achievement; stow the clothes in my car boot to deliver on my way to the supermarket for a few last-minute items. I grab my keys, and an umbrella because the skies are threatening rain, but forget to isolate Missy in the laundry as I usually do when I leave her alone.

*

She leaps from bed to window ledge – curious eyes scan the raindropped world. Kitten ears twitch at the sound of sparrows on the wet grass. She settles to lick her paw, circle her face like a motorised toy to achieve an unreachably high standard of clean. My cat is selfish, washing her body, keeping watch, lest some other cat should try to steal her place as keeper of the house.

The outstretched pale paw, testing orchid blooms to see if they are animal or vegetable, if they might fly and give chase if disturbed; the thick green leaf catching on her curving tail; the feline leap, the pot crashing to the ground, scattering petals, charcoal and pebbles, pot shards and broken support stakes all over my tiled dining room floor. Oh, Missy! Why couldn't you have broken my orchid, not Irene's?

*

Dinner is in the oven filling the house with lovely garlicky aromas when an unfamiliar car pulls into the drive. At the door before he is, I pounce on Mike with an enormous bear hug. I really don't notice anybody else at all until he breaks away from my embrace to say, 'Mum, this is Elise.'

I only realise that he is not alone at this point: am confused, but not upset, surprised but also delighted.

'But you didn't tell me you were bringing someone!' I protest. 'Lucky there's enough food for an army!'

'Elise is vegetarian,' interrupts my son. 'But some things are better said in person…Mum, Elise and I are engaged.'

The petite brunette steps out from behind Mike and smiles widely. I

give her one of my bear hugs; I haven't a clue who she is but am prepared
to welcome her as my son's partner…this is excitement beyond belief.

Mike carries in two bags as I bombard him with questions:

'Do you work together? Have you known each other long? Why
didn't you email?' Then, finally, 'But I only have a single bed in the
spare room!'

Elise blushes.

Mike sings softly, 'S, s, s single bed,' until Elise pinches him.

'Never mind, you can have my room,' I laugh. 'It is only one night.'

'I wish we could stay longer,' says Elise. 'But Mike has to fly back
on Monday. He breezed in this week and swept me off my feet with
this,' showing me the diamond ring on her finger, 'and set my parents
into a tizz, and he's going to leave me to deal with it alone.' She grins.

'Where DID you meet?' I ask again.

'Elise was teaching English in Beijing,' says Mike.

'But my contract was up, and my mother had a health scare – oh,
she's all right now – so I came home.'

'I had to come chase her,' says Mike. 'We're hoping she'll be back
in Beijing soon. At any rate, I expect to be transferred this year, might
be back to Oz, might be the States.'

'Oh, I hope you are transferred back home,' I encourage. 'We'll
have to call Susie with your news.'

'Maybe we can Skype,' suggests Mike. 'What's the time in Madrid?'

We calm down a little while Mike looks up time zones, Elise
freshens up, and I serve my homemade pumpkin soup and garlic
bread. Fortunately, I have plenty of vegetarian options – potato gratin,
roast vegetables – as well as the lamb roast.

'I found this little sweetie shut in the bathroom,' says Elise, carrying
a purring Missy. 'Is she allowed to come out?'

'She is in disgrace,' I reply. 'For breaking my neighbour's pot plant.
But she can be out on bail.'

'Poor kitty,' says Elise, settling Missy on the sofa. 'Mmm, pumpkin
soup! My favourite.'

We eat and chat. I learn that Elise's family live in Sydney's northern beaches; that she has one sister; that her policeman father and artist mother are already talking about a spring wedding; Elise is a teacher specialising in languages and music. Mike glows as we talk.

Before dessert, we pause and try to Skype Susan: eventually we reach her and have twenty minutes of family catch-up. Susan promises to try and come home for the wedding, which Mike and Elise say will happen as soon as it can be organised.

'I don't need an elaborate wedding,' says Elise. 'Marriage isn't about fashion and limousines.'

I notice the way Mike and Elise squeeze each other's hands. I like this girl more each minute.

'We could call my mum and dad, too,' Elise suggests, after we have said goodbye to Susan.

Elise's parents are friendly and as surprised by the sudden engagement as I am.

'I knew there was someone,' says her mother, Jan, 'but I didn't know it was serious.'

I invite Elise and her parents to come up for lunch next weekend to discuss wedding plans. Unfortunately, Mike will already be gone.

'Elise wants a simple wedding. Bob and I have been through it all with her sister already – we can do something similar if you and Mike agree.'

It is all such a whirl; my head is spinning as I begin to load the dishwasher at midnight. I refuse offers of help – I want a few moments of quiet to get myself together. I send them off to bed, linger feeding Missy and straightening the kitchen, laying out crockery for breakfast and locking the back door.

Elise comes in for a glass of water. 'Thank you for making me feel so welcome,' she says. 'It must have been a shock for you.'

I give her a reassuring hug. 'You might find Missy sneaking onto your bed,' I say. 'Better close the door.'

*

Today has been a blur. Last night I lay in the single bed, but of course did not sleep. Life has suddenly expanded, the possibilities are wide open, and the hope of grandchildren is beginning to blossom in the forests of my imagination. Missy nuzzled me around 7 a.m. with a cold nose, wanting food: I dragged myself out of bed and organised breakfast.

The morning passed all too soon. Mike and Elise were on the road before midday: such a short visit, but so much to think about! Elise and her parents will come up for lunch next weekend – it is all arranged. I have their address and phone number stuck on my fridge door. Missy and I napped in the courtyard after Mike and Elise had gone. Time seemed irrelevant; I was floating on another planet. I woke with a jolt around 3 p.m., my throat itchy and dry, eyes gritty.

In the corner of my vision, I saw Irene's broken pot, and the damaged orchid plant, which I had hastily swept into a cardboard carton. Motivated by guilt, I got myself together, put Missy securely in the laundry and drove to the local garden centre. I took a shard of the broken pot with me. With the help of a young male shop assistant, I found a decent match for the pot, handed over my credit card and brought it home with a new bag of orchid mix. Most of the old potting mix had fallen away into the cardboard box. I replaced it with new: at least Irene at least won't have to repot this orchid again for a while. It wasn't too damaged: in fact, in her current preoccupied state, I wondered if Irene would notice a thing. But, conscientiously, I tied a little note of apology to a stem, explaining what had happened. I believe in maintaining friendships, and not allowing any little niggle of resentment to mar conviviality. Heaven knows, friends are too easily lost, and not easily replaced, at our age. It would be too easy to let the advent of Ralph Furnace diminish our friendship – I do not want to be the one to let that happen. I finished repotting the plant and returned it to Irene's place before the evening news bulletin on the TV. I tossed the cardboard carton containing the remnants of the mess into the garage to dispose of on bin night.

I am now just settling to watch the bulletin, when the familiar theme music stops mid-cadence, the lights flicker and go out, and the sound of thunder and the flash of lightning send Missy into a furious gallop from window to window. Eventually she leaps into my arms, and we sit in darkness on the sofa, unable to contemplate our next course of action. I decide not to fumble for candles. Missy and I go straight to bed, collapsing together into my double bed, sheltering under my doona, ignoring the elements.

Deep in the bottomless fathoms of sleep, swimming underwater in the realms of unconscious desires, diving ever deeper into oblivion… how painful it is to be woken from a deep slumber! The jarring of mind and body, the sudden emergence into the present – like making landfall after a channel swim, the first steps onto dry land are shaky and uncertain, as a toddler finding her feet on an unfamiliar terrain. I hear the side gate creak. It is a particular, loud and tuneless noise. I do not ever intend to oil it; it is a useful early warning signal. Intruders? Thieves? Rumours of murderers and rapists leap into my mind. Missy hides under the bed.

I reach into my bedside drawer for the little torch that is there for such emergencies, and the buzzer that will summon an ambulance if I press it. I never have pressed it: healthier than ever in my life, I only accepted it when I moved into the village because of my children's urging. I creep barefoot, clad only in my nightgown, to the living room and look out the French door, whose curtains I have neglected to close. The storm has passed: it is a clear night now, merely some wisps of cloud scattered over the waxing moon.

There is a man in my courtyard, tall and dark. He is looking around the orchid plants, poking into corners. Looking for something. For a full twenty minutes, he searches but does not find what he is looking for. As he turns to leave, I see his face in the moonlight: it is Ralph. He doesn't see me. He leaves the way he came, closing the gate quietly. Through my bedroom window, I watch him walk stealthily over the road, back to Irene's house.

On impulse, on tiptoes I dash into my garage and shine the torchlight into the cardboard box of old orchid mix, tangled roots and dead petals. I rummage around, shining the torch into the gritty mess, until my fingers find something hard and sleek, small and cold. I pull out a little cylinder of metal, sealed with tape. I shake it but am none the wiser. I take it into my bathroom and place it in the bathroom medicine cabinet. More and more I am sure that my friend Irene is in danger, but I don't know how to help her, and can't think of anyone to tell.

*

They say that 'sleeping on it' helps solve a problem. This morning over my cup of tea, I find some notepaper and write a letter to Bob, Elise's policeman father, outlining how I came to find the sealed cylinder. I place the letter in a padded post bag, add the cylinder and address it from the note Elise put on my fridge door. Although I have only spoken with him once via Skype, my intuition tells me that Bob is a sympathetic and honest man. I badly need an unbiased opinion and disinterested professional advice. Above all, I want the cylinder out of my house. The post bag is prepaid – I was supposed to use it to send my finished illustrations to the publisher, but this is more urgent! I throw on a tracksuit and walk to the post box. Once the bag is inside, I feel lighter all over, ready to deal with whatever the day brings.

*

Of course, it is a cardinal rule of retirement village life that one should always maintain an acceptable standard of personal grooming if one ventures out of doors – there is sure to be someone else around, who will notice if your hair is a mess, your face unmade-up. In my agitation, I have ignored this maxim, going out barefaced in my raggy, pilled tracksuit and disreputable gardening shoes.

Irene hails me, cool and elegant in her turquoise and white silk caftan, accessorised with silver jewellery. (She is dressing up for that horrible man, I tell myself cattily.) 'Eileen! Yoo-hoo!'

I try to sneak around the back, but this ruse does not work. She takes my arm and propels me towards her house, insisting I take coffee with her and Ralph, 'hear their news' and 'help make plans.'

I am forced to endure the bitter brew served to me by that male snake, much too strong and not improved by the sugar I stir in, trying to make it palatable.

'We're engaged,' states Irene.

'To be married?' I ask.

'Yes, engaged to be married…silly at our age, perhaps, but Ralph feels that it's important to make a public commitment and celebration of our love.'

'Not at all,' I reassure her. 'Quite fitting. In fact, my own son…'

'We're having a party for our friends,' Irene continued. 'Then just a private marriage ceremony in Sydney. Just us and two witnesses – but not until summer. Ralph's best man – an old school chum – is away on a sailing trip and won't be back for months. Lunch on his yacht, we thought? Would be nice. We want you to be my – not bridesmaid, no, definitely not that – matron of honour, my support, so to speak.'

I try to protest, insist there must be someone closer, but no, I am the chosen one, I am needed, there is no way I can decline. Suddenly I am in the thick of two sets of wedding plans, and my attitude towards each pair of lovers could not be more extreme.

3

Misterioso

I wake with dry, gritty eyes from a long sleep, heavy and dreamless. In the pre-dawn chill, listening to the muffled rumble of the garbage truck on the road outside, I pull on my dressing gown and tie the belt tightly around my waist.

Elise and her parents are coming today: I must meet these new people, entertain them and manage polite conversation all on my own. One short meeting with Elise was not enough; I am not sure I can rely on her to smooth over any awkwardness. There is no one to help me fill any silence in the conversation or send on an errand to the shops if I have forgotten some vital ingredient for lunch. On days like this, I really wish Howard were here.

I have cleaned the house thoroughly. I have made a pavlova ahead of time: it sits in white majestic glory in Tupperware waiting to be dressed. I bought strawberries and passionfruit – I haven't been told of any food allergies, so I hope this will be acceptable. The main course will be simple: home-made quiche, garden salad.

Missy watches from a chair as I pull out the food processor, measure flour and butter, whiz pastry dough together. On all fours on the floor, I search the cupboard for my rarely used large pie pan. Missy comes down to see what is happening and sniff the cupboard for interesting smells. Impatiently, I shoo her away; she stalks off in a huff.

Pastry rolled, and into the oven to blind bake, I put the kettle on. I haven't had breakfast yet – haven't even fed Missy. No wonder she is hovering and looking put out. I sip my tea while I make the quiche filling.

The sun is up now, the morning is progressing…it will be a rush now to tidy up and be ready for the visitors. Mid-morning, they said: driving from Sydney, the traffic could be unpredictable.

At eleven, Elise pulls into the drive in her little red sports car. The man in the front must be her father, Bob; her mother, Jan, is in the back seat. Elise and I greet each other with a hug. I begin to relax.

Jan struggles from the car bearing a huge tray of home-made baklava. 'My first husband was Greek – I still use all his mother's recipes,' she explains.

Bob hands me a generous bouquet of home-grown roses.

'He's a rose-fancier,' says Jan. 'Digging around with manure and pruning thorny bushes is great therapy for a detective.'

'Oh, Mum!' protests Elise. 'She doesn't want to know all that.'

I accept the fragrant bunch of blooms and place them in a ceramic jug. I know what I will be painting tomorrow…the blush of these cream buds tinged with apricot! The dark furls of the blood-red rose…

'My first husband was serially unfaithful,' says Jan, arranging her flowing, brown linen jacket around her ample body, as she sits on my sofa and accepts a cup of coffee. 'Let's get these family history details out of the way quickly, shall we? I divorced him and settled down with Bob. Best move I ever made. Police hours are erratic, but he leaves me in peace to get on with my projects.'

Elise, sitting with Missy on her lap, rolls her eyes.

Jan is an artist, a painter of large, textured acrylic canvases and collages. A plump woman with curly brown hair, she is open and friendly. She talks about their two daughters, filling me in on Elise's background. There is no awkwardness. Bob is less talkative, but pleasant, sitting comfortably in the wing-backed chair. Missy abandons Elise, jumps up and settles on his lap. As Bob caresses the cat's head with just the right degree of familiarity, I decide that everything is going to be all right.

'Eileen…you don't mind me saying?' says Jan. 'I think I can smell something burning.'

'The quiche!' I leap to my feet, run to the oven and pull out the blackened dish.

*

'This is perfectly lovely,' Jan reassures me, as we settle down to the special of the day at the golf club bistro. 'It's nice to see part of the village, too,' she adds. 'You should bring your golf clubs next time, Bob.'

Elise has chosen a roasted vegetable salad, which looks quite appetising. Over our meals we talk about wedding dresses, colours and styles. Flowers, menus, and guest numbers. Jan and Elise are quite firmly insisting on having a garden wedding at their home.

Bob is less keen. 'So much mess and bother,' he says. 'Why not rent a hall?'

'Shush, darling,' says Jan. 'You're only worried about people trampling your rose bushes,' she says. 'It will be fine.'

Elise nods. 'Much nicer at home. No bother with cars, or bookings… You can't say no, Daddy, not when you've already done it once for Helen!'

'I'm outnumbered,' Bob admits. 'All right, chicken.' He gives Elise a peck on the cheek. 'In for a penny, in for a pound. Thank goodness I've only two daughters.'

I've been ignoring the fact that Irene and Ralph have come in from the golf course and are shouting drinks at the bar.

'A hole in one!' Ralph is saying, giving a blow-by-blow description of his triumph.

Irene sees me and gives a little wave but doesn't come over.

'Will you have bridesmaids?' I ask Elise.

'Most likely two school friends,' she replies. 'We really have to pick a date so that I can make sure they're in the country.'

'Young people travel so much these days,' remarks Jan. 'Globetrotting on a whim. I never had the money at their age.'

Bob has fallen silent. I look over and see him paused, part-way through his seafood platter, surveying the room.

He says quietly to me, 'Eileen, who is that dark-haired chap at the bar?'

I know he means Ralph. All the other men in the room are bald or silver-haired. 'My neighbour's fiancé,' I reply. 'Ralph Furnace.'

Bob shakes his head. 'He's bad news.'

*

I don't let my guests order dessert because I have a perfectly good pavlova waiting for us in my kitchen. Elise and her mother walk ahead; Bob and I stroll behind.

'What did you mean?' I ask. 'About Ralph?'

'That isn't the name I know his face by,' Bob says. 'I shouldn't really discuss it, but I'm sure it's him. That man – he has various aliases – is wanted by the federal police. He hasn't been living here long, I'd guess. He's only recently met your friend?'

I nod. 'I'm worried about her.'

'…and he was the man searching in your courtyard at night?'

I nod again.

'And you think he hid the cylinder, that you posted to me, in Irene's pot plant?'

Another nod. My throat is dry and my legs feel wobbly.

'Stay away from him. And from her, if you have to.'

'But…'

'I can't say this strongly enough: don't trust him an inch.'

'What was in the cylinder?' I have found a voice, but it doesn't sound like mine.

'All I can say is that it's still being tested. And…please, you must stay away from that man.'

*

Irene hires caterers for her party, but she still wants my help choosing dishes, decorations, calculating quantities. She sends Ralph around hand-delivering the printed invitations. By the end of the day, he has charmed every silver-haired widow in the village. (My hair is stubbornly brown, even if it comes from a bottle, and will not be fooled.) I must help her shop for an outfit, flowers, even a gift for Ralph.

While we are alone shopping, I try to gently hint that it is all so sudden; ask her what she actually knows about Ralph; and why don't they simply get to know each other better before making such a commitment?

'There is no time to waste at my age,' Irene states in a matter-of-fact tone. 'Don't spoil this for me, Eileen! I never had anyone of my own. Let me enjoy this romance, this belonging, while I can.'

I hold my tongue and worry silently about my conversation with Bob. I am supportive choosing fripperies and making suggestions about colours and styles. At last, most of the arrangements are made, and I plead exhaustion. I also have a commission to finish. This buys me two days of relative peace, so that I can think about Mike and Elise, and my own plans.

Missy is restless, needy, curves her sleek body around my legs and rubs her jowls on my calf. I sit on the sofa. She nestles in for a cuddle as I stroke her head. The rhythmic motor of her purring throat calms me, helps my thoughts to a greater clarity. I decide that if I really must attend Irene's wedding, I will drive myself, stay somewhere separate from the wedding party. That way I will be less constrained by Irene's wishes; can arrive for the ceremony and depart as soon as I can. I will not travel with them in their new Mercedes (the BMW proved unreliable) as Ralph had suggested. Independence is required. I'm really hoping to wriggle out of attending the wedding somehow. An illness? But in the meantime, I must play along. There is one other difficulty to be faced: what to do with Missy while I am away?

The thought of a cattery is unpalatable. Joan and Larry? No, Larry is allergic to cats. The only person who I think would be open to the idea of a feline house guest is Annette; but Missy does not take well to her. I wonder if it would work? I can't think of any alternative. Feeling like a traitor, I reach over the cat's sleeping body for the phone and call Annette immediately. She is only too happy to help; loves cats; will either visit twice daily or take Missy home to her house, whichever I prefer.

'Let's work out the details at Irene's party,' I say. 'Will you be there?' I ask mischievously, referring obliquely to Annette's very early routine bedtime.

'Yes, I will be there,' said Annette. 'I feel Irene needs as much support as I can give her…taking on such a change at this time in her life.'

'She may need friends more than we know,' I agree, hoping I am wrong, hoping that by some miracle Ralph will simply disappear as quickly as he came.

I'm in the shower getting ready for the party when the phone rings. I let it go, thinking I will never reach the bedroom to answer it in time, but it rings out, and then starts again, so I jump out and grab a towel, and in doing so slip on the tiled floor, wrenching my left ankle. Hobbling to the phone, I curse whoever is ringing, causing me to drip water and shampoo bubbles onto the carpet.

'Mum, MUM? It's Susan,' says the voice, strange at first, then unmistakably my daughter.

'What a surprise,' I laugh. 'I've just sprained my ankle getting to the phone.'

'Not really? Oh, Mum…hope you haven't broken anything.'

'No, no,' I say. 'How are you?' I sit on the bed and chat with my daughter about inconsequential things, gossip about Mike and Elise, and I tell her about Irene and Ralph. I tell her about his past, what Bob said, everything I suspect. She is the first person, other than Bob, I tell about my suspicions, the first release for the pent-up worry I have been carrying around like a lead weight in my chest.

'That's awful,' she says.

'I have no proof,' I reply. 'And Bob might have been mistaken. People look different in photographs, don't they? I'm just a silly old woman imagining things.'

'Hardly that,' says my daughter. 'Be careful, OK?'

*

35

I phone Annette. 'Are you walking around to Irene's? Will you come via my place? I've done a silly thing and wrenched my ankle… I'd be so grateful for someone to walk over with…walking stick? Oh really? Well, I've never…it couldn't hurt…yes, oh, thanks SO much.'

I choose a pair of sensible flat shoes and strap up my ankle with layers of crêpe bandage. When I am finished, it looks much worse than it actually is – sure, it hurts, but nothing that a day or two won't heal. I am going to have a tailor-made excuse to leave the party when I have had enough of that smarmy Ralph.

Annette arrives at my door holding a wooden walking stick. 'It was my father's,' she explained. 'I keep it for situations such as this.'

Missy leaves the sofa and circles Annette's legs, rubbing her little face on Annette's black velour trousers.

'Sorry,' I say. 'You'll end up with white cat hairs all over your outfit.' I can't understand it; Missy is usually so standoffish with Annette.

'All part of the plan,' says Annette, taking a small plastic bag from her pocket. She unzips the bag, takes a morsel of sardine with her fingertips and feeds it to Missy. 'More later,' she tells the cat. 'Oh, all right, just one more now,' she says, feeding her again, then putting the rest back into her pocket.

Laughing, I take Missy to the laundry for the night, pick up the walking stick, and hobble with the solicitous Annette across the road to the party.

*

Irene and Ralph greet us at the door with kisses.

'New perfume?' Ralph asks Annette.

'What HAVE you done?' asks Irene, eyeing my foot.

'Nothing really, just a sprain,' I explain. I have bandaged myself comprehensively so that Irene cannot examine my injury with her doctor's skill. 'Just lead me to a chair and pour me some of that champagne.'

'Can you smell fish?' Irene whispers. 'I'm sure I didn't order any fishy canapés. Ralph's allergic to sardines. Hope the caterers haven't messed up.'

'Annette, come and sit with me,' I say. 'I want to tell you all Missy's little habits. Annette is kindly going to look after Missy while I'm in Sydney,' I explain.

'Blasted cat,' says Irene. 'Always a bother to have animals. Such a tie.'

'Pets and husbands,' says Annette. 'Life is much easier without either.'

'But less fun,' I smile.

Irene heads off to check her caterers, Ralph hands me a flute of sparkling wine. Annette asks for lemonade. As Ralph serves it, he sneezes violently. Once, twice…and moves away before the third explosion.

As soon as he is out of earshot, Annette hisses, 'I really can't bear that man.'

I take a large swig of champagne. I look Annette directly in the eye and see genuine concern.

'I'm very worried that Irene is making a terrible mistake,' Annette continues, grasping my forearm with a trembling hand. 'I don't like to speak out of turn, but I've seen…and heard…things…that worry me dreadfully.'

'Perhaps this is not the right place,' I reply, looking around the room full of chattering party guests. 'But I do understand. We should talk. Tomorrow?'

'I'd be so grateful to confide in someone.'

I put my own hand over Annette's trembling one and give the cold fingers a reassuring squeeze. 'Come over in the morning,' I say. 'Pretend it's official orchid business, if you like.'

*

'I'm so glad I'm not coming to Sydney with you,' Annette says as she hands Missy a morsel of sardine.

The morning after the party, we are ensconced in my cosy living room, with mugs of hot chocolate and macaroons Annette has brought. I have my ankle elevated, because it is a little swollen and bruised, but really, not too bad.

'How so? I thought you loved weddings.'

'That awful man,' Annette says, looking over her shoulder in the direction of Irene's house, as she lifts a compliant Missy to her lap.

'What has Ralph done to annoy you?'

'Neither a borrower nor a lender be, that's what my parents always taught me. He asked me to lend him money. A really large sum. I was so upset… I haven't been able to sleep without saying an extra prayer for Irene every night.'

'You surely didn't agree?'

'No, of course not. I didn't come down in a shower of rain yesterday. But I think perhaps Irene has not…made a good choice.'

'Just between you and me and Missy,' I reply, 'I think you're on the money.'

'That's not all,' Annette continues. 'Don't know if you've heard? There's been a spate of burglaries up in the hostel. Cash, jewellery, small items taken from rooms…the staff are in a complete uproar because they're all suspected. But I can tell you that this has only happened since a certain person and her fiancé began volunteering.'

I knew that Irene and Ralph had recently become community-minded and now help with the book trolley and activities programme in the hostel. Irene had described how she would help frail residents choose reading materials; obtain favourite snacks, do any personal errands. Ralph, she had claimed, was so good at conversing with people, he often lingered behind chatting, and she had to round him up to finish their visit. How large are his pockets? I wonder. How dare he steal from those helpless old dears!

'That is appalling,' I state, putting down my half-eaten macaroon. 'But how could we ever prove it is him?'

'I don't know. But there is one really sad item that's missing,' says

Annette. 'Mrs Enderby – you know, Alice Enderby – she turned ninety last month? She has kept her grandfather's gold pocket watch. Quite a valuable antique: a family heirloom. Recently she had it restored and she's been showing it around. She was planning to give it to her son on his own birthday this year. The watch has gone. I saw her show it to Ralph Furnace the day we had community singing with the church choir in the hall.'

'Last week? That was last week?' I ask. Community singing is not something I get involved with.

'Yes. Thursday last week. I was so upset when Mrs Enderby told me the watch was missing. I helped her search all through her room. It is definitely gone.'

'We need a plan,' I say. 'We need to get Irene and Ralph out of the house so that I can search for that watch before he sells it.'

'Could we really? How could we…?'

'Would you ask them to do some urgent volunteering for the next bus picnic?' I suggest. 'And I'll plead my sprained ankle as an excuse.'

'Yeees…there is one planned for next week. I don't mind a little white lie for a good cause…but how will you get in?'

'Don't worry about that,' I reply. 'I have a key.'

*

'I've come to check on your ankle,' proclaims Irene, as she breezes into my living room. She has used the spare key, has not knocked or asked permission to enter. 'I don't think you take proper care of yourself.'

'Nonsense. I've been resting it all day,' I say, bristling at the intrusion.

'Have you been for an X-ray?' she asks.

'No. It really is just a sprain, Irene.'

'Let me take a look.'

'Oh, no,' I protest.

'I insist,' Irene replies. 'I would never forgive myself if it was fractured and I hadn't helped you. Can't be too careful at your age.'

Feeling very annoyed (I am, after all, younger than she is) nevertheless I allow Irene's deft fingers to prod and manipulate my ankle.

'Do you have any pain?' she asks. 'Does this hurt? And this?'

'Yes,' I reply truthfully. It does hurt. If she starts asking me to rate the pain on a scale of one to ten, I shall let her have it.

'Mild swelling, but just a sprain,' Irene reports.

'Just as I said.'

'Keep off it for a while. But not too long. Do you see a physio?'

'Irene, don't fuss. It will be perfectly all right in a day or two.'

Irene fidgets with the diamond ring on her finger.

'How is Ralph?' I ask, to change the subject.

'Keeping busy, as always. You know we've been asked to help with the bus picnic? Volunteering does take a lot of time and energy. But Ralph is so good with people…I understand why they asked him especially… I can't think why you and he don't get on.'

'He's not good enough for you, Irene.' As soon as the words are out of my mouth, I bite my tongue.

'Never thought you'd be the jealous type!' exclaims Irene. 'Just because you're alone, and I've found a soulmate…'

'That's not it at all,' I reply. 'If he were an honest man, I'd be so happy for you. But he isn't, Irene.'

'You don't know anything about him.'

'I know more than you think.'

'Made-up lies and gossip.'

Irene tosses my ankle, which has been resting on her lap, roughly to the floor. I wince.

'For my sake, you should try and get along,' says Irene. 'Please don't spoil this for me.'

'Let's have a cup of tea,' I suggest. I do not want to fall out with her. I get to my feet.

'Sit down, sit down…I'll make you some tea… Really Eileen, you have to think of others more…spending your time cooped up with your stupid cat instead of mixing with people…'

Irene fills the kettle noisily and sets about washing up the few dishes I had left in the sink.

'Don't Irene. I'll do that later,' I protest.

'Nonsense. I'm here to be neighbourly and help. Which is what you should do more of. Why aren't YOU helping with the bus-picnic?'

'But my ankle…' I begin.

'So, it is disabling when you want it to be, but not when others try to help…'

'Irene, that's hardly fair.'

Irene finishes by serving me a very milky cup of tea with sugar in it. She knows I don't take sugar.

'Put it there on the table,' I request.

She sets it down, slopping the overflow onto the saucer.

'Thank you,' I say pointedly. 'I hope you and Ralph enjoy the picnic.'

Irene leaves as swiftly as she came. As the front door clicks shut, Missy's head pokes out from under the skirt of the wing-backed chair.

'Coast is clear, Missy.' I lean over and pour some of the sweet, milky beverage into the saucer, place it on the floor. Missy doesn't mind a bit of sugar.

*

Annette drops in every day, ostensibly to check on my sprained ankle, which is now quite healed, but actually to go over the details of our plan. 'I feel just like I did the time Father caught me stealing licorice all-sorts from the shop,' Annette confides. 'Deliciously mischievous.'

'Shop?' I inquire.

'My parents had a corner shop, mixed business, when I was a child,' says Annette. 'I used to help serve after school. I loved liquorice. And there was a big jar full – I didn't think anyone would notice.'

'Just like Ralph,' I say. 'Thinking no one will notice his crimes. Well, he'll find out that we're not all old codgers who don't see what's happening under our noses.'

'I was punished by having to give out free sweets to all the children who came to the shop, and not have any myself, for a whole month.'

'I hope Ralph gets into much more hot water than that, when he's caught,' I state emphatically. 'All this trouble we're going to, to get the evidence.'

'Irene didn't want to go on the bus trip at all, but I laid it on very thick, said that we needed extra people to manage with the wheelchairs. We're leaving at ten, and we'll stop for a picnic lunch at the dam, be back by two in the afternoon. That should be long enough…'

'Oh yes,' I reply. 'There can't be that many hiding places.'

'He wouldn't carry it with him?'

'If that's the case, you'll have to search his pockets,' I tease.

'Push him in the dam and then he'd have to strip,' says Annette.

'Great idea!' We laugh. 'But it might sink to the bottom of the dam.'

'At any rate, it shouldn't come to that. I hope you'll find it hidden in his sock drawer.'

The day of the picnic is fine: from my bedroom window, I watch the picnickers set off in the minibus, laden with a trailer full of wheelchairs and mobility aids, food and drink. There are so many people going, several cars follow behind: one of these belongs to Irene and Ralph. I am dressed and ready: I have found a pair of rarely worn soft leather gloves in my drawer. A bit melodramatic perhaps, but no sense in leaving fingerprints when there is no need. I collect the key from the Spode sugar bowl in the china cabinet; put my charged mobile phone in one pocket in case of emergencies, and my digital camera in the other. At quarter past ten, Annette sends a text message to say that all is well, and the coast is clear.

'Well, yes, I can see that for myself,' I tell Missy. I have a slight headache, perhaps from nerves – it doesn't feel right to be trespassing on Irene, even if in a good cause.

I look anxiously up and down the street – best not to be observed going into Irene's place – and walk swiftly over, let myself in the front door, close it quietly behind me.

A mechanical noise coming from the dishwasher in the kitchen; a drip, drip from the shower; and someone has left the radio on in the bedroom. Must have left in a hurry. Where do I start? I wonder.

Bedroom. Following Annette's advice, I check each drawer. Much silk underwear, belonging to Irene: cashmere socks, cotton boxers, nothing hidden there. Bedside tables hold moisturising creams, massage oil, reading glasses, a manicure set.

Wardrobe: more of a challenge. Most of the space is filled by Irene's things; only a fraction holds men's clothes. A few man-sized shoeboxes: I check those first. Nothing. Up top are more boxes: but I will need something to climb on. First, I decide to check the pockets of Ralph's jackets. In each of them, I find various amounts of cash – adding up to a significant amount – but this is not useful evidence. Anyone could have money in their pockets. At the end is a suit in a zippered bag – for the wedding? I wonder. I take this out, and unzip it, searching the contents. Eureka! In a money belt hidden in the bottom of the suit bag, various rings, some set with old diamonds, some plain gold bands, some brooches and watches. Just the sort of things that have been taken from residents of the hostel. I spread them out on the bed and take photographs, before putting them back. In the inside pocket of the suit jacket I find a gift-wrapped box the size of my palm. Wedding present for Irene? Mrs Enderby's pocket watch? Should I unwrap it?

Hesitating, I suddenly become aware of another noise apart from the dishwasher and the radio. A car has pulled into the drive. I freeze. I watch from the window, my heart pounding, as Ralph walks to the front door, swinging his keys in one hand, mobile phone clutched in the other. Frantically, I close the bedroom door and turn the key that is fortunately on the inside. For good measure, I wedge a chair against it.

As swiftly and quietly as possible, I pack away the suit, the radio noise giving me a little coverage. I hear Ralph's heavy footsteps in the hall: then his phone rings.

'Rachel?' he says. 'Where are you, honey? I thought you were meeting me at the house? No, Irene isn't here… I made an excuse to leave her at the picnic… No, she won't…you're being silly… Oh, all right, I'll come to you in town… It's just a waste of precious time…' As he talks, he walks out of the house.

After he has driven away, shaking, I reopen the wardrobe and remove the package from the suit pocket, sit on Irene's elegant cream bedspread to unwrap the mystery.

*

'It wasn't the watch at all,' I moan to Annette. 'After all that, it really WAS a wedding present for Irene.' I show her the photo on my camera, of an antique pearl choker, set with diamonds and sapphires. I had taken comprehensive photographs, including the front and back of the jeweller's box that held the choker nestled in satin. I don't know why I did this: habit, I presume. A botanical illustrator takes many reference photos from many angles, to get the details just right.

'But you found all the other things,' reminds Annette. 'Which proves he is a thief.'

'Yes, but not the pocket watch,' I complain. 'I really wanted to find that for Mrs Enderby.'

'Wait a minute!' exclaims Annette, looking more closely at the photograph. 'Allen's Antique and Estate Jewellery,' she reads. 'Precious items bought and sold. You know what that means, don't you? I bet he sold the watch to this jeweller and bought this for Irene. Or did some kind of deal. We should visit this shop.'

She reads out the address, a shopping arcade in a nearby inland town, and I jot it down on the back of an envelope. We arrange to go next morning. Annette says she will drive. I want to discuss the whole thing with Bob but decide to wait and see what we find out at the jewellery shop. I don't want to confess twice about our amateur sleuthing. He is sure to disapprove.

*

'I feel rather excited,' confides Annette, as we drive out of the village next morning in her little white hatchback. It is a blustery day, and she had arrived on my doorstep wearing a copious Marple-esque tweed cloak, red woollen gloves and knitted beret. For driving, she adds dark glasses, as the winter sunshine is very glary. If she had decided to dress up as someone in disguise, it wouldn't be more obvious: but it doesn't matter: people in the village are used to Annette's singular outfits. They wouldn't think anything of it. And I might convince her to remove the cloak once we reach the arcade.

Since it is cold today, I have worn my leather gloves, remembering to keep my arthritic fingers warm. My ankle is much better, almost normal, but I have worn my ankle boots, which give it maximum support. I have a long cashmere scarf wrapped around my shoulders, to keep out the wind.

As we leave my house, I see Irene trying to sweep up leaves on her driveway. A bit useless in this wind, I ponder. Ralph, too, is dressed for gardening. He holds open a large garbage bag, and Irene tries to gather and deposit the leaves inside it. I wave to them as we drive off.

I haven't been in Annette's car before. It is far from new, but scrupulously maintained. The windscreen is spotlessly clean. I think of the dusty film covering my own car and feel ashamed. Annette is a precise but jerky driver, zooming along to traffic lights and coming to an abrupt stop; changing lanes and travelling at speed with a businesslike demeanour.

We arrive in good time and find a parking spot in the main street. The arcade is a two-level, quasi-Victorian building, with iron-lace and stained-glass windows. An 'Olde Tea Shoppe' is at one side of the entrance, an antiques and old wares bazaar on the other.

'We can have coffee,' Annette suggests. 'After we've seen the jeweller.'

'Unless we need to make a quick getaway.'

'Why? Do you think Ralph will show up?'

'No, I'm just being silly,' I reply.

'There's a yarn shop too,' observes Annette. 'And a boutique. Let's give ourselves some cover by checking those out first.'

I go along with this suggestion, purchase some unusual homespun wool in the yarn shop, with a pattern for a woolly hat. If Susan doesn't want it, I can always give it to the craft stall at the village fete. Annette tries on a mustard-coloured dress in the boutique, but I talk her out of buying it, despite it being heavily reduced.

'It does nothing for your colouring,' I remind her. 'You're much better off with a warm splash of colour, like your scarlet beret,' I insist.

'Well, you ARE the artist, so I'll take your advice,' Annette agrees. She buys a red blouse instead, which is not reduced, but it will give her much better service. 'Now for the jeweller,' she decrees.

I feel an unreasonable fluttering in my stomach as we push open the heavy glass door and hear a little tinkle of the bell above us that alerts the owner to customers. He takes a while to appear from the back room, but we can see him through the window in the connecting wall, sitting at his bench, working on a watch. We survey the items in the display cases, taking our time, admiring the rings and brooches, bracelets and pins. There are some very nice pieces. How much of it is stolen property? I wonder.

When the jeweller comes to the counter, I ask to see a little pearl and opal ring, which looks like something Elise would enjoy. I don't know her ring size, but I could have it altered… I slip the glove from my right hand and try the ring on my own little finger as Annette asks about watches. The ring is loose on that finger, so I remove the dress ring I am wearing on my ring finger. It is only a cheap-but-cheerful ring I picked up at a local craft market, a piece of broken porcelain mounted in white metal that may or may not be silver. The pearl ring is still too large on that finger. I decide it won't do for Elise.

'Do you have any antique watches?' Annette asks. 'I want to buy one for my nephew's twenty-first birthday. A pocket watch. You know…with a chain?'

'Ye,s indeed, madam. Just a moment.'

While the man – Mr Allen, I presume – leaves us to bring out the watches, I lean over to Annette. 'I didn't know you had a nephew!'

'Shh…I don't.'

'What will we do if he has Mrs Enderby's watch?' I whisper.

'Buy it back, of course,' Annette hisses. 'Hush, here he comes.'

Mr Allen opens a velvet roll and shows Annette three pocket watches, two silver and one gold.

Annette picks up the gold one and gives a significant nod to me. 'This one is lovely,' she says. 'What price?'

The jeweller names an amount that makes me gasp.

'Will you hold it for me?' asks Annette. 'With a small deposit? I'd like to check with my family first. May I take a photograph to show my sister?'

Mr Allen agrees, writes a receipt for Annette's deposit, allows her to take a photo with her digital camera, then takes the watches back to his inner sanctum.

Well done, Annette, I think. You are a better liar than I dreamed.

Annette takes a look at the tray of rings on the counter. I remove the pearl and opal one from my finger and place it back in the velvet slot.

'Hmm…I love these old rings,' Annette says. 'That one looks just like my mother's engagement ring… I still have it at home, although I never wear it…' She stretches out a tentative finger to touch the square-cut solitaire. She suddenly plucks it from the tray and examines the inside. 'This IS my mother's ring! See the engraving? The date and her initials! How did…when did…? That Ralph Furnace will rot in prison before I'm done…'

I take the solitaire ring from her. While the jeweller's back is turned, I slide it on my finger and replace my glove. I put my cheap ring into the empty slot in the tray. Annette stares at me, open-mouthed.

'I'll meet you in the tea shop,' I call as I leave the room, bell tinkling above me.

*

The special of the day in the Olde Tea Shoppe is cappuccino with cinnamon rolls. Annette orders some: I am already on my second double-shot latte.

'Why did you do that?' asks Annette when the waitress is out of earshot. 'Now WE are the thieves. I had to linger chatting, just so he wouldn't be suspicious.'

'Not we, ME,' I reply. 'I just felt so angry. It is YOUR ring, after all.'

'But now we can't prove Ralph stole it,' Annette says.

'We still have Mrs Enderby's watch as proof. This was just the last straw.'

'Should we be stopping here?' Annette asks. 'Mr Allen might notice the ring you left and come looking for us.'

'I'll blame it on extreme age and poor memory,' I assert. 'We're just a couple of poor old dears who made a mistake.'

'Perhaps he'll just call the police.'

'If he is dealing in stolen property, would he call the police? I don't think so. It depends what story Ralph has told him. Hey, why don't you wear your mother's ring from now on, and make sure Ralph notices. Shake him up a bit.'

'No, I want to catch him properly,' replies Annette. 'Don't want him to evade prosecution.'

'It's time to bring in the professionals,' I sigh.

I take my phone out of my handbag and call Bob for his advice. He sternly advises us to go straight to the local police station and tell all. He will be in touch.

*

For several days after our visit to the jewellery shop, Annette and I wait smugly for the police to arrive and cart Ralph Furnace away. I keep vigil by my front window, and Annette is a frequent visitor, but nothing happens. My ankle is quite healed, so I tell Annette to keep in touch by phone instead of dropping by, because Irene has noticed her visits.

'Seeing a lot of that Annette lately, aren't you?' she remarks one day, as we chat by my letter box.

There was a postcard from Mike amongst the bills and circulars, and I had paused by the drive to read it.

'She's been so kind, dropping by in case I need any shopping or help because of my ankle,' I explain.

'Well, some of us offered our professional expertise, and were rebuffed,' complains Irene. 'Pride goeth before a fall, you know.'

'It was just a slight sprain. It really wasn't worth all this fuss,' I say. 'And I do appreciate all my friends. More than you know.'

For more than a week, Annette and I wait, and I am sure Missy does too, and sitting in the window, watching, ears alert. Nothing escapes Missy. In the end, I can wait no longer, and phone Bob.

'May I drive up to see you this weekend?' he asked. 'Jan will come too. It's a very complicated case, lots that I have to explain, and it'll be better done in person.'

*

I have never been that good at secrets. My mother could always worm them out of me; and whenever I tried to plan a surprise for Howard or the children, I was always found out. So when Bob tells me, over grilled salmon and salad in my courtyard, that I must keep some information confidential, even from Annette, it is rather a trial.

I plead to be allowed to tell her. I doubt my ability to bear this knowledge alone. All through lunch I worry. I serve pavlova for dessert, and cut my thumb slicing strawberries.

Jan notices my agitation and tries to convince Bob to agree that Annette be in the secret.

'You can tell her that Ralph is a known criminal, that the petty thefts here are just part of a much bigger picture,' Bob says, taking a second helping of pavlova. 'But I don't want you to talk about the canister you found. We need to keep stringing him along for a bit longer, gather more evidence, before he's arrested.'

'Poor Irene!' I exclaim. 'What can we do to protect her? How can I just let it go on…'

'You're being a better friend to her than she'll ever know,' Bob asserts. 'This pav is really good, Eileen! The best thing you can do for Irene is to keep quiet, go along with things, be vigilant, until the police are ready to act. Ralph, as the suspect calls himself now, always marries the women he targets before he…'

'Before he murders them! How many have there been? Oh, Irene!' I can't help the tears that are now falling on my cheeks.

Bob looks around uncomfortably. 'If the strain is too much, perhaps you should go away for a while, take your mind off it.'

'You could come and stay with us,' suggests Jan, with an encouraging smile.

'No,' I decide firmly. I wipe my eyes with the napkin Jan hands me. I must stay and keep an eye fixed on this villain. He doesn't know it yet, but he has met his match in Mrs Rickaby.

After our long lunch, Bob goes for a walk around the village. 'Excellent meal,' he says. 'Need some exercise. That's Irene's house over there, right?'

I nod. I make some commonplace remark to Jan about the health benefits of walking.

'He gets antsy after meals since he gave up smoking,' explains Jan. 'So instead of lighting up, he walks. It's his thinking time, too, he says.'

We gather up used dishes and stow them inside the dishwasher, give Missy some fish scraps, boil the kettle for tea.

'I'd love to see some of your botanical paintings and illustrations,' says Jan. 'If you aren't shy about them? Elise told me how skilful you are.'

Despite the way I have crammed all my painting gear into the spare room to clear the dining table, I take Jan in, stepping over boxes and manoeuvring around my easel, show her some finished work, and a couple of orchid paintings I have on the go. She admires the intricacy of the work; we chat about paper and pigments, art suppliers and venues for selling work.

'I exhibit in a local gallery,' she says. 'But I don't sell much.'

Missy leaps up with a mighty swoop, onto the spare bed on which we are sitting, not wanting to be left out of the conversation. I pet her; she settles down between us.

'My best sales have been from the local homemaker centre,' Jan continues. 'I supply a large canvas to match each lounge room setting, to hang over their fake mantelpieces. Often the buyers will want something for their wall, and either buy the one displayed, or commission something similar.'

'Illustrations are my main money-spinner,' I reply. 'But I don't do enough to call it an income.'

'I know what you mean. I just make enough to buy more paints...'

We hear Bob come in the front door. 'Any more pavlova, Eileen?' he calls.

I make the tea and serve Bob another helping of pavlova. Jan laughs as I abstain, saying I want to trim down for the wedding.

'No chance of that for me,' she says. 'Anyhow, it would spoil my day job.'

'Day job?' I ask.

'Life modelling,' Jan replies. 'I have a reputation as the best, full-figured life model for the local art societies and painting schools. Keeps me in pocket money. But don't tell my daughters.'

Bob looks over at me and gives a slow wink.

4

Ritenuto

I have a hedge around two sides of my little courtyard, a hedge of white camellia sasanqua. I love the pure, delicate flowers, even though the petals drop so fast there is no point in cutting them for a vase. It grows so well, I need to trim it each year, otherwise I would be hemmed in a jungle of my own making. This sunny morning, I decide THE TIME HAS COME and I get out my sharp garden shears and a little stepladder, so that I can reach the high spots, and begin trimming.

I've only just completed the first side when footsteps and voices down the side path indicate that visitors are imminent, and Missy flees into the house from the warm spot she has been enjoying on the sun lounge.

'You look busy,' says Irene, holding hands rather immaturely with her beau. 'So glad your ankle's fully healed.'

'Yes, just trimming the hedge,' I reply. 'Sit down and I'll get us all a drink. I could use a little rest.' I would rather keep on going and get the job done. But one does have to be neighbourly, and there is bound to be a reason for this visit. I may as well be comfortable while I discover what they want.

We agree on coffee, so I go inside to brew some, and give Missy a little food to keep her inside out of harm's way. I have seen Ralph nudge her roughly with the toe of his expensive leather loafer when he thought I wasn't looking. Not a cat lover: doesn't surprise me in the least. Villains never are.

Returning to the courtyard with a laden tray, I find Irene seated comfortably at my small bistro café table, directing Ralph. 'Just a bit more on that branch above your head,' she instructs. 'No, not that one, to the right.'

Ralph is up the stepladder, hacking at my camellia.

'Oh no, please stop. Come and have coffee,' I beg. 'I'll finish it later.'

Ralph takes another vigorous swipe at my hedge with the shears, leaving a hole large enough for his head to poke through.

'Please make him stop,' I implore Irene.

'Ralph, dear, come and try some of this slice Eileen makes. It's to die for!'

Irene manages to coax him down, and I sigh with relief, sipping the coffee that I have made extra strong. I lean back into my chair and wonder what favour or task I am about to be pressed into. I am sure there is a reason for this unscheduled visit. I close my eyes and take another mouthful of hot coffee, letting the caffeine soak into my cells, storing up fortitude for whatever comes next.

'It's like this,' Irene begins.

My I-thought-so expression must have shown in my one raised eyebrow, because she simpers and begins again.

'It's like this, Eileen. You are the most trustworthy of friends and the nicest, most reliable neighbour I have here in the village. You are the only one we can possibly turn to.'

I take up my dark glasses, which I had temporarily laid on the table, while making coffee. Better to hide behind something, even something as insubstantial as these chain store shades.

'We have decided,' Irene continues, 'that my villa isn't big enough for two people. Ralph needs a den, and I've never shared a house with anyone. I have a great many things that take up too much space.'

I nod, although by my standards, Irene's house is uncluttered and minimalist to the extreme. I wait.

'But we love the location, the convenience, the people…' Ralph adds. 'So I'm going to purchase one of the larger villas being built on the other side of the golf course.'

I know about them, had looked, like everyone else in the village, at the plans on display in the community centre. The houses are more like suburban mansions than homes for downsizing retirees. Four bedrooms, en suites, stairs…not at all what elderly folk require, in my humble opinion. But then again, Ralph is not yet seventy. Perhaps he will do all the running up and down stairs when Irene can no longer manage it. I nod again.

'Trouble is,' says Irene, 'all Ralph's money is currently tied up in overseas investments, and it will take time to access the required funds. I'll sell my villa to pay the deposit on the new house. But it isn't easy to sell these smaller villas quickly, although the centre management says there is a steady demand over time…'

'We know you'are particular about your neighbours,' smiles Ralph. 'So we thought we'd give you first option. To buy Irene's villa. And rent it out, or sell it on, to your approved purchaser.'

Speechless, I nod again.

'Then you're in favour of the idea?' Irene asks.

'Yes…I mean no.' Shaking my head for emphasis. 'NO…I can't buy your house. Although I see your desire for a larger place. But I can't help you. I don't have the money…'

This is not quite true. Howard had a good superannuation fund, and I have never travelled or spent much. I shake my head again. I can't believe Irene doesn't have the money for a deposit herself, without selling her villa.

'A bridging loan?' asks Ralph.

'You could do that, Irene,' I suggest.

'No, I already…' begins Irene, but Ralph covers her hand in his larger, tanned one, and for the first time, I notice the heavy gold signet ring on his hairy finger. She stops mid-sentence.

'Perhaps you…?' he suggests.

'My parents taught me never to go into debt,' I assert. This was not quite true – we had borrowed money many times to manage my long-distance swimming commitments – but it was always honourable and above board. There was nothing honourable about Ralph, I was more certain of that than ever.

I stand to pour more coffee, but don't sit down again. I reach for my hedge shears and begin snipping at foliage above Ralph's head. Some of the leaves fall into his cup. I notice a thick green caterpillar on the hedge, pluck it off and lay it on the table. 'Must do something about these pests,' I reflect aloud, taking another swipe at the camellia.

*

Early next morning, Ralph comes to the door. I am in my dressing gown and slippers; although I have showered and done my hair, I have not yet finished dressing. My security screen door is locked. I don't open it.

'Aren't you going to ask me in?' he asks, well-manicured fingers reaching for the door handle.

'I have a cold,' I lie. 'Better that you keep your distance, don't catch it.'

He laughs and swings the rolled-up morning paper he is carrying, like a baseball bat. 'Takes more than a cold to slow down old Ralph.'

'Did you want something?'

'It's about your cat,' he leers.

'About Missy?'

'Keep her out of our rubbish bins,' he demands.

'Rubbish bins? Missy never…'

'There was a cat, just like yours, in our bin last night. Screeching and caterwauling, scratching and pulling everything out. Made a terrible mess…flathead bones and prawn heads everywhere!'

'Missy is never out at night.'

'I tell you, it was your cat.'

'Describe it.'

'A pure white cat, just like yours, blue eyes, white feet…'

'Missy is not pure white, Mr Furnace. She is blue-pointed. And I always keep her indoors after dark. Good day.' I close the door on him, so angry that I am shaking. Once again, I wonder, how Irene can want to marry such a man?

Next day, Ralph appears at my front door again, this time holding a bunch of supermarket daisies. This time I am dressed and presentable.

'I thought I'd look in and see how you are,' he says.

I know that the daisies are a ploy to make me open the door. But what choice do I have? Without being absolutely rude. Politeness so ingrained in us, it becomes automatic, a habit. Of course I open the door, accept the daisies, and murmur thanks. He's through the door and into my living room before I can blink.

'How is Irene?' I ask.

'Irene? Well, very well! An appointment at the hairdressers this morning. I dropped her in town. I thought I would be neighbourly, make sure your cold hasn't worsened.' Ralph is walking around the room, surveying the details like a real estate agent.

'No worse, thanks,' I reply, taking a tissue from my sleeve to dab my nose.

'Great! Any chance of some of that excellent homemade slice? And coffee?'

Against my better judgement, I fill the kettle and arrange mugs on a tray. 'Go through to the courtyard,' I say. 'I'll bring it out there.'

'Excellent!' says Ralph. 'May I help? No? In that case…may I use your…? Wash my hands?'

Without my permission, he slips through to the bathroom and closes the door. I am sure he is checking the medicine cabinet, searching for the cylinder. He won't find anything.

I make the coffee extra strong, hoping the bitterness will send him quickly on his way. As an afterthought, I add a half a teaspoon of salt to the pot. I take the tray to the courtyard, then stand in the hall, waiting outside the bathroom door for Ralph, and then usher him outside. He is not going to have any chance to pilfer *my* jewellery from the bedroom.

'You've lived here…how long? Eileen?' he asks.

'Since my husband died. I downsized.'

'And you have children?'

'Yes. Two.'

'But not close…'

'We are a close family, but my children are both working in important jobs overseas,' I reply defensively. 'We talk regularly on the phone.'

'Travel much?' he asks.

What is this? Sixty questions, I think to myself. 'No, not often,' I reply.

'Saving, not spending, the children's inheritance,' Ralph smiles. 'If you ever want in on a good investment opportunity, I can steer you in the right direction.'

I thank him perfunctorily; pour more of my bitter brew into his mug.

I take the opportunity to ask about his work; where he has lived; his family. He gives very little detail away. He is a master of general statements, impressions without facts. He eats all the slice I have laid out on the plate. Missy looks at me through the glass: she is sitting on the living room windowsill, looking out.

Ralph sees her too, and comments, 'Such a lovely thing, a pet, for companionship. You must be careful, though – I saw a little kitty just like yours on the side of the road this morning, squashed flat. You could see the imprint of the tyre on her poor little body…'

Missy leaps from the windowsill, and I know that she has run and hidden under my bed.

'Missy is an indoor cat,' I say. 'She is perfectly safe.'

After a painful half-hour of forced conversation, I let him out the side gate. I throw the bunch of wilting daisies into the bin. I lock up the house and sit with Missy on my lap. She has been hiding but has now reappeared with all the sympathy in the world in her blue, blue eyes.

I turn on the radio. There is a concerto playing: just the thing, a bit of Mozart to calm us down. We snuggle together and let the music fold over us like a soft blanket. Before long, Missy is asleep and I, too, am dozing off.

A screech of tyres on the road outside disturbs us both. A few minutes later, there is an insistent pounding on my front door.

'Who is it?' I call from the hall, holding Missy in my arms. 'Who's there?'

'Police,' comes the gruff reply.

I take a moment to put Missy in my bedroom and shut her in. I open the front door just a little.

The burly man in jeans and black T-shirt standing with his hands on his hips certainly is not a policeman. I keep the security door shut tight.

'Where is your identification?' I ask.

'Don't worry about that, luv,' leers the man. 'I need to see Mr Furnace.'

'No one by that name here,' I reply. 'You must have the wrong house.'

'No, this is the street, and the number – he give it me on the phone, right? So you just go and get him, right? He's your son or somefink, right? You tell him I said game's up, Ralphie.'

'There is no one here of that name,' I state, calling on all my resources of dignity and ending up sounding like a 1950s newsreader on the ABC. 'Leave this house immediately, before I call a real policeman.'

I daren't suggest he go across the road to Irene's house. I don't want to set this thug onto her, even if I wouldn't mind seeing him give Ralph a bit of what is due him.

'Lardy-da! You ain't seen the last of me, lady,' he says, kicking a booted foot against my screen door. But he goes, he stomps away and jumps onto the motorbike that waits for him in my drive, and speeds off, revving the motor much more than required around the bend and out of the village.

*

I phone Annette to confide about the bikie visit. I admit to being a bit shaken. She and I have a long talk, which calms me considerably.

'You must call the police,' she advises. 'The local constabulary as well as your Bob.'

Although Annette has yet to meet Bob, she is quite taken with the idea of him. I can see her making up romantic fantasies of him stepping in to save Irene in the nick of time.

'Yes, yes, I will,' I promise.

'And keep your mobile phone in your pocket,' she continues. 'Have you got Bob's number on speed dial? Better be safe than sorry.'

After talking to Annette, I do go and charge up my mobile, which has been lying neglected in my handbag. I call Bob on the landline, describe the thuggish features of the bikie all over again. Bob calls the local police, who send a car round to patrol the area.

Two polite young constables arrive some time later and I describe the bikie once more. I am not sure whether my description is getting more lurid with each telling… This time, I remember the writhing tattoos on his neck…the smell of garlic that emanated from his person, and the nicotine-stained teeth that grinned at me through the screen door. Perhaps I am letting my imagination run away with me? Or does memory become keener under pressure?

After the police have gone, I check the house again, making sure all the doors are locked and the windows secure. The phone rings: it is Annette.

'Would you like me to come over and stay the night?' she asks. 'I don't mind sleeping on the sofa.'

'No, no, I'm perfectly all right,' I reply. 'No need, really.'

'You could come here if you prefer,' she says.

'I'm not going to let it worry me,' I reply. 'I'm quite safe and sound. More worried about Irene, in case those thugs, whoever they are, work out where Ralph really is.'

'Good night, then,' says Annette. 'Don't let the bedbugs bite.'

I run a bubble bath, but before I can get in, my mobile phone beeps with messages from Susan. I turn off the taps and have a long gossip with my daughter. Her common sense helps put everything into perspective.

At the end of the conversation, I let the water out of the tub and have a brisk shower instead. With a hot drink and Missy on my knee, I watch the late news on TV. As the weather forecast is read, the phone rings. It is the local police, saying that a group of bikies have been arrested during a scuffle in town, during which a Mercedes was vandalised. One of the men matches my description. They reassure me that the man is in custody and will not be able to make trouble for any local residents.

'There, Missy,' I say, tickling the cat under her chin. 'Everything will be just fine.'

*

Next morning, Irene phones. 'There are some workmen making a dreadful mess of our footpath,' she complains. 'Tools thrown around everywhere. Just wanted to warn you so that you don't fall over a shovel when you go out.'

I thank her and ask if she knows what they are working on.

'Broken pipes, I think,' she replies. 'Although in a recent development like this, you'd think they'd be all new.'

'Nothing is made to last any more,' I reply. 'Or maybe it's a different kind of pipe – you know, something to do with internet and broadband.'

'Noooo, I don't think that's what they said,' she replies. 'And I can't see any logo on their uniforms. Must be contractors of some kind. Anyway, be careful, and for goodness sake don't fall over their mess and break a hip.'

'Don't worry about me, Irene,' I say. 'I can look after myself.'

After we finish talking about Orchid Society business, I go to the window and look out. There are four men in fluorescent jackets standing around a hole over which a tent-like screen has been erected. A mould of clay from the hole they have dug is heaped over Irene's front lawn. One of the men takes a walkie-talkie from the low-slung belt on his hip, talks into it, adjusts his hard hat. Another man hands him a steaming beverage from a Thermos.

'I think the cavalry has arrived,' I whisper to Missy.

I am out in my front garden sweeping the path when Joan and Larry walk by pulling golf carts, on their way home from a game. They are both licking ice cream cones. I ask about their game; remark on the fine day. Last of all, I ask about the cones.

'Yes, there's been a Mr Whippy van circling round the golf course most days this week,' Larry observes. 'Lots of people buying cones instead of drinks after the game. The clubhouse must be suffering. Although I must say, the bloke hasn't a clue how to use the machine properly.'

'Must be new to the franchise,' suggests Joan, taking a lick. 'We've never had an ice cream van come around before. He's doing a roaring trade.'

'You've got workmen here too,' says Larry. 'We've had tradesmen crawling all over our place, reading the gas meter, checking the fuse box…'

'Must be some sort of maintenance drive,' says Joan. 'We must find out at the next residents' meeting.'

'There's a curry night at the clubhouse,' says Larry. 'How about coming along with us?'

Although I know Missy will be put out, I agree to tag along with them.

'We'll come by at six,' says Larry.

*

Joan and I choose beef curry; Larry goes for curried prawns and saffron rice. Over a congenial meal, we discuss the goings-on in the village. I am tempted to confide my concerns about Ralph but decide to put it all out of my mind and have a carefree evening. Larry goes to the bar for wine: while he is gone, Joan asks about my children. We talk about Mike and Elise, weddings and grandchildren, have a pleasant chat.

Larry is gone a long time: when he comes back, he is arm in arm with Irene, and Ralph is carrying a tray of drinks. Irene and Ralph pull up extra chairs and join our table, which makes it rather crowded, as it is only designed for four people. I am the fifth in a group of two couples. Gooseberry, I tell myself.

Ralph places a large jug of lager on the table, and two bottles of wine. 'A red and a white,' he says, 'to cover all the bases.'

Joan looks put out. I know that she doesn't like Larry to drink too much, as she is worried about his health. Neither she nor I will have more than a glass, but with Ralph already pouring, it will be hard to keep within sensible limits.

'Drink up, Joan!' says Ralph. 'Plenty more where that came from.'

'I'll be away next week,' confides Irene, who is sitting beside me.

'You and Ralph going somewhere?'

'No, Ralph will stay and look after the house. You needn't worry about the plants. I'm going to fill in for a colleague at the hospital in Sydney.'

Irene hasn't done any locums for quite a while: I thought she had done with all that. Surely it isn't for the money?

'Won't Ralph be at a loose end without you?' I ask.

'Oh, no, he'll get in some serious golf,' Irene replies. 'It's only for a few days.'

'Are they very short-staffed?'

'I'm doing it as a personal favour,' Irene states. 'A very dear friend asked me particularly. And you know, I find it hard to let anyone down.'

'I hope it won't tire you out,' I say. 'Just when you're really enjoying your retirement.'

'I always want to stay in touch, be useful and help out when I can. My years of experience shouldn't be wasted. I'm thinking of joining a mentoring programme for young graduates...'

'As well as your overseas work?'

'Yes. The pro bono scene is one thing; but actual participation in my own local system is just as worthwhile.'

'You must be so proud of Irene's skills,' I murmur to Ralph.

'A toast to professional women!' cries Ralph, raising his glass. 'Long may they reign over us!'

'A toast should be in champagne,' objects Irene.

Ralph gets to his feet. 'I'll be right back,' he says, heading for the bar.

*

A session of trying on potential mother-of-the-groom outfits in a small boutique in a neighbouring town has left me feeling blobby and discontent.

Driving out of the town centre back to the village, I notice the sign for the you-beaut aquatic centre. It opened last year; I remember the hoo-ha in the local papers. Wonderful amenity for the local schools, the youth, the disabled, the… Sounded much too busy for the likes of me, I was always a solitary swimmer. But on impulse, I turn my little car into the side street and the freshly tarmacked car park, and easily find a parking spot near the entrance. Not so busy, after all.

The bright royal blue and turquoise interior is neat and reassuring; there is no unpleasant smell of chlorine or fast food odours. A small, tidy café overlooks the children's pool, complete with artificial palm trees; the Olympic pool is to the side, and the timetable on the wall indicates dedicated lanes for lap swimmers at certain times of the day. It is all so unobjectionable, I go into the small swim shop and purchase a pair of ladies' racers, bathing cap and goggles. I have already noticed the complimentary towels.

Before ten minutes is past, I am steadily ploughing up a lane in the Olympic pool as if I had never had a day's rest from training. I will be a svelte mother of the groom, and not only that, my mind will be clear and calm, with a deep serenity only the influence of water can produce. Howard knew this and encouraged me to swim while the children were small and demanding. I have forgotten myself in my rush to join other widows in the retirement community, forgotten the need I have to be immersed in the buoyancy of mind and spirit that only comes to me in a solitary swim. My muscles are tired but pleasantly so: I know I shall sleep well. I feel home at last.

*

The next Orchid Society Meeting was to have been at Annette's house, but at the last minute she cancelled, so Irene offered to host. This was out of character, especially as Ralph was staying, but maybe Irene wants him to get used to our village ways, or maybe she just isn't thinking, or…who knows what is in Irene's mind these days? Certainly not me. I miss our quiet conversations and glasses of wine in the early evenings. Not that she is neglecting me, no. I have more invitations than I want, to sip wine with her and Ralph. No, three is a crowd, and Mrs Rickaby is better in solitude than on a gooseberry bush.

At any rate, I tidy myself up this sunny afternoon and walk across the road, laden with a date loaf (store-bought, I am afraid) and notes for the meeting, including the schedule for the orchid show which I had promised to draft.

'Come in, come, in,' says Irene, answering the door. 'Everyone is already here. Coffee? Tea? 'She takes the date loaf and hands it to Ralph. 'My beloved is looking after the eats,' she says. 'Let's rip through this agenda so we can enjoy ourselves.'

The reading of the minutes from last meeting takes rather longer than it should. Annette is absent and the fill-in secretary stumbles over the idiosyncratic wording Annette has used. Leslie Wilde, one of the men on the committee, takes exception to several points which need to be changed.

I distribute the draft schedule I have brought and take a handful of cashews from the dish beside me on the sofa table. Unfortunately, one of them sticks in my throat. I leave the room in agony to fetch a glass of water from the kitchen.

There is a young woman facing the door, facing Ralph, who stands with his back to me. His full attention is on her, as the kettle steams full bore on the bench between them. I stand, motionless, in the arch of doorway, my hand clutched to my throat, and realise something had been about to occur.

Her hands hold the two undone ties of her wrap-around dress at ninety degrees to her body, her dress aloft like the sails of ship about to catch the prevailing wind. I do not stop to take in her exposed bosoms, her curving belly, only partly concealed by a half-wrap of her dress. I stride in, take a crystal glass from the counter and fill it from the cold water tap. I leave with the glass in my hand just as silently as I entered. No words are spoken by Ralph or the woman. She reties the dress over her heaving breasts.

It is up to me to covertly ask Irene, as I sip my water back in the living room, 'Who is that woman with Ralph in the kitchen?'

It is all I can do not to laugh out loud when Irene replies, 'Rachel is Ralph's cousin. She's on her way down to Sydney to start a new job and she's staying a couple of nights in the motel in town.'

I don't have to reply because at that point the woman in question comes out of the kitchen carrying strawberry scones and is generally introduced to the members of the Orchid Society committee. Ralph carries a bowl of clotted cream, to go with the scones.

'Do you see much of your cousin?' I ask Ralph innocently as he passes plates around.

'Not as much as I'd like,' he replies.

'She's very handy in the kitchen,' I observe. 'Obviously a very talented girl.'

There is general relief that the official business of the Orchid Society has been dealt with. Everyone is happy to linger over afternoon tea, and the conversation becomes quite lively and playful. Someone suggests a meal at the local Chinese restaurant.

'Oh, yes!' says Rachel. 'I saw the sign in town. They have karaoke.'

'Let's all go,' encourages Irene. 'We haven't had a night out as a group for ages.'

It is all spur of the moment stuff and, swept along by their enthusiasm, I go home to change and settle Missy with some tuna, so she won't be too put out about my leaving her alone. I don't go out much at night these days, but once in a while, it does put some verve in your step, to find that favourite black velvet evening jacket and put on a little lipstick, slip on some gold-trimmed shoes and be driven into the town and enter a fairy-lit restaurant with friends.

We settle down to a banquet around a large circular table. I am seated beside Ralph and Irene, opposite Rachel. Rachel has not changed; she is wearing the same wrap-around dress, which slips open from time to time and needs frequent adjusting. I suppose she hasn't brought many clothes with her on such a short trip. The air conditioning is quite cool, and I think of offering her the cashmere wrap I had grabbed leaving the house, but on second thoughts, decided it would interfere with Ralph's view. He is obviously enjoying the show. Irene is absorbed in the menu: then we discuss details of printing the *Orchid Society Journal*, which had somehow been neglected at the meeting.

The soft background music ceases, and a sudden electronic blur of notes announces the beginning of a karaoke session. A couple of regulars, amateur singers but tuneful enough, from another table begin with standard songs. There is an audience singalong with everyone as we progress from spring rolls to satay skewers.

Ralph bounds up, takes the microphone and gives a surprisingly good rendition of 'Till I met you'. He finishes by kissing Irene's hand, and I admit that even I am charmed by his act. Another of the Orchid Society members has a go at a Carol King number; then Rachel seizes Ralph's hand for a duet. Like Sonny and Cher, they face each other on the small stage wiggling and pouting as they sing 'I Got You Babe'.

Something on the menu hasn't agreed with me: I go to the bathroom with an upset stomach and get an early ride home with another couple. Missy is watching for me on the front windowsill. It takes two hours of the classical radio station to get that annoying song-worm out of my mind. Two more hours of reading before I hear Irene drive home. There is only one set of footsteps on her front porch.

I phone Annette the next day, to see if she is OK, after missing the Orchid Society meeting.

'…just a little medical problem,' she says.

'Your arthritis playing up?'

'Nooo…a mammogram result…just a little doubt about the findings…got to follow up.'

'Oh, Annette, I hope it's a false alarm.'

'Thank you. I appreciate that. But I'm not talking about it to people generally. There is breast cancer in my family, you know.'

'I'm sure it will be OK. What about we do something just for fun? Take our minds off this and all that other business with Ralph. It's half-price at the cinema today.'

'Hmmm…that is a kind thought… Yes, you know, it could be just what the doctor ordered.'

'Pick you up at 1.30? For the afternoon session?'

'Thanks, Eileen. Give Missy a cuddle for me.'

'Will do. See you soon!'

Life is full of trouble, I reflect, as I busy about tidying my kitchen, and check the paper to see what film is showing at the local cinema. Watering my orchids, I think about all the friends I have lost to cancer. Too many to number. 'We must make every day count,' I tell Missy, as the cat stalks a butterfly in the courtyard. Missy swats the air and misses the colourful wing by a millimetre. She sits and basks in the sun. I am totally sure that Missy has understood exactly what I am talking about. Annette should have a cat, I reflected. A little companionship does us all good.

*

'Do you have any family, Annette?' I ask to fill a silence in the conversation as we drive to the cinema. 'Brothers and sisters?'

'I was an only child,' says Annette. 'Left to my own devices. My parents were always working in the shop. I played behind the counter, dressing dolls in clothes I made from empty sugar bags. My toys were the weights and scales for measuring flour… I was so proud when I was tall enough to really use them and serve customers.'

'Me too. An only child.' I think about those childhood days when I seemed to be the centre of my parents' world: early swim sessions, long drives to competitions, sensible meals and impromptu singalongs in the old Holden.

'Were they musical? Your parents?' asks Annette. 'Did your love of the classical pieces come from them?'

'Ah…I don't know. My mother played…'

I remember how she would lift open the burled-walnut lid of the upright piano, curve her work-worn fingers over yellowed ivory keys and begin a tune. I close my eyes and listen. What was the melody she always played? My eyes flash open in sudden recall. Of course, it was *Weigenleid*, 'The Cradle Song'. I remember her taking my small hands and putting them on the keyboard, slowly tapping out the tune. We didn't get very far. I wasn't a good pupil, so those informal lessons were soon overtaken by swimming and school. How would my life have been different, if I had taken up music instead of swimming? Would I still have lost my parents so early?

'Yes, I guess the classical music obsession must have come from Mum,' I say. 'But I lost her so young, it's hard to say.'

Most of the house contents belonging to my parents had been sold. On Aunt Mabel's advice, I kept the set of Spode china, the family photograph album and my own clothes and books, when I moved to her house. I don't know what happened to the piano, who bought it. I don't know what other clues to my parents' personalities and pasts may have been lost in the clearance. Dad's car was damaged beyond repair and went to the scrapyard. Somewhere in a country town there is a double grave with a simple marble headstone. Aunt Mabel chose the words: At rest. I have never visited it.

To change the subject, I ask Annette about her favourite movies.

'For me, no doubt, it's *The Sound of Music*,' declares Annette. 'All those wonderful songs… I still rely on it to lift my spirits whenever I'm down.'

'Yes, musicals are great for that,' I agree. 'But my favourite films aren't musicals. I like a drama, something to keep you guessing…'

'A whodunnit?'

'Yeees, or even a love story when the end's in doubt…' I turn the corner and drive into the car park.

'Too often it's just blood and guts and a predictable plot.'

Fortunately, there is a new release movie showing today, a light story with an ensemble cast of British actors. A happy ending that will encourage us. By the time the credits roll, and we have wiped our fingers, sticky from the choc-tops we have consumed, on capable Annette's disposable all-purpose wipes from her capacious handbag, we are in a cheerful state of mind.

Leaving the theatre, we follow the crowd of matinee patrons to the exit, and I notice a familiar profile in front of me. I am pretty sure it is Rachel, Ralph's 'cousin'.

She is talking on her phone. 'But you promised…you said you would meet me this afternoon! I can't wait around for you, forever, Ralph. You have to…yes, I know…I *am* being patient…I'm leaving today, and you won't see me again until it's all over. Yes. Yes…no, I don't love you…well, just a little bit…no! I can't say that!' She looks around but doesn't see me. 'I adore you,' Rachel says into her phone.

I hurry Annette to the car. As we buckle our seatbelts and reverse out of the parking space, I feel a bit distracted and annoyed. The feel-good effect of the movie has been spoiled.

'He got me drunk,' Annette blurts out.

Rain is beginning to fall. I switch on the windscreen wipers and drive out of the car park. 'Sorry?' I ask.

'He got me drunk. The father of my baby.'

'Ohhh…' What has brought out this sudden confidence?

'At a dance. A one-night stand, they'd call it these days. I was staying with cousins in Victoria. Never tasted beer before.'

'In Victoria?'

'Uncle had a sheep station. My cousins took me along to a dance in town… I only had one partner…we went outside for a drink, it was so hot, a humid night, I remember that much…and a walk to the creek… I must have passed out – and woke up alone in the brown dust with my best frock covered in vomit. Never saw him again.'

'Oh, Annette.' The rain is heavier now. I turn up the wiper speed.

'A shearer, I think…never really knew –'

'You had to face it all alone.'

'The nuns called me a dirty slut. Mum and Dad sent me away until it was all over, never talked of it.'

'People can be cruel.'

'I was damaged goods, like the stale bread in the bin outside the shop,' Annette says. 'Worthless. I worked for nothing for years. Couldn't go back to school. Then I got an apprenticeship with a milliner.' Annette wiped a corner of her eye with her index finger. 'I was good at that, made wonderful racy styles with feathers and chiffon, sweeping brims…but no one wears hats, these days. Millinery is a lost art. My life, in a nutshell.'

The rain is now so heavy, visibility is very poor. I am glad to turn the familiar corner into the village.

'I got a letter,' confided Annette, opening her handbag, withdrawing a long blue envelope. 'From my son.'

'Your baby son? Does he –'

'Not a baby any more. A grown man with a daughter of his own. And he wants –'

'To meet? Will you?'

'I'm so afraid!' Annette thrusts the letter into my lap as I stop the car outside her house and pull on the handbrake. She bows her head and holds her age-spotted hands to her face.

I scan the typed letter. There is a picture attached. I hold the small photograph close, examine the placid face of the middle-aged man. 'He looks perfectly lovely,' I say. 'What have you got to lose?'

'He might be like Ralph,' Annette sobs. 'Just after my money…'

'…or he might be like you,' I say. 'Just a decent, normal person.' I hand back the letter, reach over and give my friend a hug. 'Not all men are evil.'

'You were lucky –'

'Yes, Howard, bless him, was –'

'Trouble is, I don't have anyone to be with me, in case –'

'I can be there. I can hover outside when you meet,' I offer. 'And call the police if he looks dodgy.'

Annette laughs. 'Yes, I am being silly. I know I should be happy… but it's all so long ago. He'll want to know about his father, ask so many questions I just won't be able to answer. And I won't know what to say or what to do…'

'Sleep on it,' I suggest. 'You'll know what to do tomorrow. Climb every mountain…'

Although the rain is easing, Annette slides a navy-blue folding umbrella out of her sensible handbag, pops it open and walks briskly under its shelter to her front door. She turns and waves, shakes the umbrella dry as she goes into her well-lit hall.

The windscreen glitters with droplets, but the rain has ceased. I drive away, humming. Missy will be waiting.

*

The day after the movies, and a night full of strange dreams, I am late to get moving. My routine is out of whack. I don't get to the aquatic centre at my usual time, and find that an aqua-aerobics class is taking place at one end of the lap pool. Although I have already changed into my swimmers, I am about to walk away and leave, when a couple of the women in the pool resting on fluorescent-coloured noodles recognise me and call out my name.

'Eileen! Eileen Rickaby! Come and join in!'

Politeness demands that I walk over and converse. I have to explain that I want to swim laps, and that I don't do aerobic classes, but the women insist, and before long I am beside them in a splashing, swirling mob of mature ladies, moving to the bouncy sounds of seventies pop music. I vow that I will never be caught like this again.

After the class, I deftly dodge the instructor's efforts to sign me up for next week. I go to the change rooms with the others to dry off and change.

As one plump lady pulls off her bathing cap and shakes out her grey curls, she turns to me and says, 'I am glad to run into you, Eileen. You know, I'm really worried about your neighbour.'

She has my attention immediately. 'You mean Irene?'

'Yes, Irene. That man she's involved with – Ralph Freeman.'

'You mean Ralph Furnace.'

'Nooo…Freeman. Ralph Freeman is his name, dear.' The woman, whose name I simply cannot bring to mind, towels her torso vigorously with a souvenir beach towel from Fiji.

'I'm all ears,' I prompt.

'My cousin, second cousin actually, knew his wife. In Queensland. It was all very strange. Suddenly she – Mrs Freeman, not my cousin – was said to have cancer, and they went overseas for a cure…'

'But she died.'

'Yes, she died, and she was cremated overseas, and he brought back the ashes. They held a lovely memorial service, but my cousin thought…we all thought…there was something fishy.'

I nod.

'And next thing you know, her house is sold, all her assets left to him, although they were only married a year and she had three children from her first marriage, who got nothing. Their entire inheritance, poof! Into smoke. Nothing that their father, a really lovely hard-working sort, you know, had scrimped and saved for them, nothing left. We were all so angry.'

'I'm so glad you told me this,' I confide. 'I don't think Ralph is good for Irene at all.'

'Of course, there's no proof of anything,' she continues. 'But if you can find any way to warn Irene…give her a little hint…'

'Love is blind,' I say. 'I wish that Irene would listen to me, but she's infatuated.'

'I will pray for her,' says the woman, whose heavy gold cross glints on her drop-covered bosom.

'I'm very much afraid that's all we can do,' I say. 'Irene won't take notice of anything I say about Ralph.'

A few days later, at a loose end, I walk over the road to visit Irene. Ralph is screwing a bracket on the wall. He is wearing a loud floral shirt, unbuttoned, exposing his hairy torso. Irene's expensive abstract painting of Sydney Harbour, which I much admire, has been taken down and is casually propped against the dining table.

Ralph heaves a flat-screen TV into position.

'What's going on?' I ask. 'Nice shirt.'

'The shirt was a thank you present from Rachel,' says Irene.

'She's gone?'

Irene nods.

'And the TV?' I ask.

'A present from Ralph,' says Irene.

'Oh, I didn't know you were interested in…'

'I've needed a larger screen for some time now.' Irene states. 'Kind of Ralph to organise it for me.'

'Need a man around to do these things,' Ralph agrees, playing with the remote control.

Until now, Irene has been perfectly content with her small bedroom TV for current affairs and travel documentaries, the only viewing she enjoys.

'…couldn't see the ball on that tiny screen of hers,' remarks Ralph as he tunes into a cable channel showing golf.

'Foxtel as well?' I remark, raising an eyebrow at Irene.

'Got to have something to while away the winter evenings,' she says.

'But surely –'

'Can't get any volume,' complains Ralph.

'Where'is the manual?' asks Irene.

'Haven't got one,' says Ralph.

'Where's the box?' I ask. 'In the recycling? I'll find the manual.'

'…no box, no manual,' growls Ralph, examining the batteries in the remote.

'How so?'

'Floor stock,' says Ralph.

'Come on, Eileen, let's leave him to it,' says Irene. 'I want to go to the nursery for seedlings. Will you come?'

Gladly, I leave Ralph to sort out his technology. As we leave, I hear him curse the TV and kick a chair. A deafening blast of the theme from *Hawaii Five-O* emanates from the house. I hope the painting survives his ranting. I should have told him what it was worth. It would probably have been gone when we got back, but at least it would have been safe from damage.

As we look at pansies and petunias, choose a colour palette for Irene's garden border, I decide to comment on Ralph's taste in televisions. 'Those large screens really dominate a room,' I say. 'Hard on anyone not interested in watching.'

'Relationships are all about compromise,' declares Irene, picking up a punnet, inspecting the underside for root growth outside the container. 'You ought to know that…or have you forgotten?'

This little dig about my widowed state does not miss its mark. I finger a frond of Queen Anne's Lace. I try again.

'Some men are more dominant than others,' I begin. 'Howard, bless him, was –'

'Yes, I know, your Howard was a saint. But the rest of us have to make do with mortal men. Perhaps you should look around for one of your own, instead of living in the past?'

Ouch. I enjoy the small friendships I have with men in the village, on the orchid committee, passing the time of day with neighbours, but I certainly have not thought about living with any of them. I am content, just me and Missy, and Irene knows it. She is being unkind.

'Let's have a coffee,' I suggest, steering her to the garden café. As a gesture of reconciliation, I pay for the refreshments, and keep the conversation light and breezy. There's nothing to be gained by arguing with Irene. There will be no way to help her if we are at odds with each other.

For a while, life in the village goes into hibernation. Many residents have taken trips to find some warmer weather. School holidays come, and that takes more people away to visit distant grandchildren. Irene and Ralph are self-absorbed, are involved in golf games and I barely see them come and go: Annette has a touch of flu and stays indoors watching DVDs of *Carousel, Showboat* and *The Sound of Music* for company.

I hunker down too and finish the illustrations I have begun for a couple of publications. Then I have nothing left to do, feel a bit at sea. I tidy up my painting supplies, toss out some scraps of unfinished work. I can't feel inspired to begin anything new. I begin a library book, but find that, although the cover is different, I have read the novel before – it isn't interesting enough for a second reading. At a loose end, I find myself standing at the fridge, nibbling at chocolate-covered sultanas left from Christmas; snacking on pretzels at the open pantry door. I could easily lose myself and track of time, eating odd things at odd hours, but Missy keeps me on track. She indicates, by a swish of the tail, an urgent meow, or a gentle paw, when it is the official time for meals. So I make myself a proper dinner each evening, share it with the cat, and go to bed on schedule.

I have ramped up the heating in the town house, because even though we have a mild climate, winter seems to have really settled in this year. Walking outside is unappealing, and there is no one about to chat to on the lonely streets. I begin knitting the homespun wool I purchased that day with Annette, and think about the situation with Irene and Ralph. It can't go on much longer, surely? Something must happen soon!

I notice that I have been purling when I should have been doing plain. I pull down the stitches and begin again. I go to the fridge and get the jar of chocolate-covered sultanas. I spend the afternoon knitting, nibbling and listening to Dvorak on the radio. The violin is keening, like a weeping woman. The melody carries the sort of melancholy that resonates with known sadness and releases old troubles from an aching heart. And whisks them away with the final flourish of the conductor's hand.

I wonder if Mike and Elise will have children. Whether one day I will be one of those grandparents jetting off overseas to visit little ones. Will I be a good grandmother? I haven't been around children for so long, I will be very much out of practice. Perhaps the joy of holding a newborn babe, whose DNA you share, is enough to buzz old hormones into life and bring back mothering skills long forgotten?

I am starting to get into the rhythm of knitting now; the pattern is not really that hard, if you concentrate… The afternoon wears on and the light dims. I reach over and turn on the table lamp, keep knitting, to finish the last rows of the hat.

'Yes, Missy,' I say aloud, as the purring cat drapes her body around my calf. 'I promise I will do something about dinner soon.'

5

Agitato

Half awake, half nestled in a dream, I roll over to my left side, stretch out my arms, invite Howard to slide between my thighs, to rock with me on our private ocean of ecstasy. He isn't there.

Of course he isn't there.

I roll further, to the empty side of the bed, lie prone against the mattress, feel the firm cool flatness against the length of my body. Eyelids closed tight over the forming tears, I push my head against the yielding pillow, wishing I was still asleep. Wishing I was not alone. I will not stay long in this position: my lower back will rebel. I roll back to my normal sleeping position, on my right side. Eventually, curled like a foetus, I doze again.

My dreams are of swaths of cool silk slipping over warm, young skin…of laughter, shyly revealed pink nipples, fingertip caresses the full length of my bare arm. Of youth and recognition; of matching desires and familiar needs. I am the solitary swan, who mated for life and lost her partner to the hunter's gun; I am the gosling imprinted with the image of one nurturer who cannot find belonging with any other.

The soundtrack of my dream is nothing like the controlled tones of the classical radio station. It is the hot pulse and swirl, the energy and impatience, of dance music. The sound of the dance halls in which our romance was enacted. These melodies and dormant passions flare up now and then, like a neglected snow globe shaken and tipped upside down to release a flurry of movement. What unseen hand has prompted this surge of feeling? I have not willed it to arrive, sought it, or nurtured it with longing. Irene is wrong when she says I am living in the past. I am doing my utmost to stay grounded in the present, to stay in control and not be swallowed by this never-ending grief. I have played the measured melodies of Mozart and Handel to keep me calm and serene. I have maintained good sleep habits, sensible diet, regular exercise. I have not lingered over faded photographs or wished for days long past: yet here I am, weeping again over my lost love. Howard, I love you. I miss you. You weren't perfect, but you were mine.

Missy wanders in: she has been elsewhere, probably checking her bowl in the kitchen. She doesn't approve of all this tossing and turning. She leaps up onto my bed and circles around. Sniffs the doona. I have disturbed her nightly repose: she is thinking of another nap.

'Don't settle in, Missy,' I say. 'You know it's time to be up and about.'

She looks at me with solemn blue eyes.

Howard's eyes were blue. As blue as the sky that announces another day to be lived without him.

*

'Click on the PDF icon,' instructs the local history librarian. 'Then you can view the service history of your very own ANZAC!'

Obediently I click on the icon. I don't have any war heroes in my family. I have looked up a distant cousin but I'm not really all that interested. Trying to fill these anxious days, I have come with Joan to a seminar at the library on researching your family history. But now I am wishing I was at home with Missy.

I take a surreptitious look at my watch: twenty minutes to go. I click around on the web page, leave the war record section of the online archive and go into the general family history pages. I look up my father's birth record, then my grandmother…and realise with a start, I don't know her maiden name.

Joan, an experienced family history researcher, guides me to locate my father's marriage details. My grandmother's maiden name is recorded, and her place of birth.

'Now you have something to go on,' Joan smiles.

I work through the documents, discovering family members I have never heard of, the names of great-grandparents, their parents…it is overwhelming.

I click back to begin a new search and enter 'Ralph Furnace'. Nothing. I try 'Ralph Freeman'. The only matches are a Queensland man who died in 1933, and a Tasmanian born in 1825. I check my spelling. I consult with Joan. There are no birth records for Ralph, under either name.

*

After the library session, Joan goes off with Larry to do their weekly shop. With no place to go, no errands or shopping to be done, I drive aimlessly to a local park. It is deserted: no mothers or toddlers playing in the quiet, green spaces, no little hands floating leaf-boats on the pond. I guess the children are all at cafés, drinking babyccinos, playing electronic games. I feel vaguely guilty, here alone, like a schoolchild playing truant. Skipping out on all my responsibilities. If only I knew what they were. I am like a car, idling in neutral.

I walk to a seat made of bent willow, sheltered within a small arbour, and watch the birds – red-eyed crows, finches, cockatoos grazing for grass seed.

A wagtail flies in. He dances on the fence, the rockery, the pavers around the yellow irises. The tree, the rock, the pond. I listen to the conversation between the wattlebirds and the wagtail. The chime of bellbirds. Birdsong is generally considered to be peaceful, but today their chattering suggests a whole subtext of disagreement, territorial squabbles, mating rituals and other bird business I can't even imagine.

I close my eyes and imagine the pond life swirling below the meniscus of the water. I feel the twinge of unknown insect life crawling on the bare skin between the straps of my sandals. I think of the slaters, beetles and worms living below the leaf mulch.

They say the wagtail carries our secrets. Forgotten secrets. The secrets of our hearts. Those pieces of the jigsaw lost forever, leaving blank spaces that can never be filled in. The family group posed for a photograph beside their motor car in dustcoats and wide-brimmed hats, names lost to memory. As nameless as beetles and unknowable as the birds.

Birds hide their secrets way above our heads: we cannot see into their nests or stickybeak into the cracked, spotted shells to see which life has been saved and which aborted. The butcherbird will not confess.

If I could only adjust my hearing with some kind of digital bird translation microphone, I would be able to understand the tweets and the natters, the whistles and the twitters. Birds have been witness to the whole mess of mankind – what couldn't they tell us about our secret histories?

If only I could send a bird to spy on Ralph Furnace, Freeman, or whatever his name really is. A scavenging crow: to discover his real background, report on his evil doings, or even peck his eyes out.

Ants bite my feet and I worry about what else might be lurking in the pine bark. The whistles and calls don't warn me; they are meant for species of a different feather. How precious my babies were to me. How I loved them. And now I must nut out my future, fill in the blanks, as best I can. In the drawer of Auntie Mabel's oak sideboard there had been a box of unused, yellowed, deckle-edged notepaper. A pair of pinking shears. One five-pronged piece of iris petal, from the corner of the jigsaw puzzle. I didn't look any further. I took a few obvious family pieces as keepsakes and called in the second-hand dealer to take away the rest. What will Susan find in my house when I am gone? What should I remove and what should I leave?

*

I try not to visit the doctor very often. There's nothing wrong with me – apart from a little arthritis. I listen to my friends and neighbours go on about their appointments, tests and ailments: leave me out of it please. I can't bear medical conversations. But occasionally, I go:

have routine blood tests, allow the doctor to advise me about regular exercise, diet and sleep habits. It doesn't hurt to have someone take a kindly interest in you, now and then, when you have no one in the house but a feline companion. Makes you feel a little bit that you might matter to someone, after all.

My ankle does ache from time to time, although the sprain is healed. I feel on edge: a restlessness I cannot shake. I am waiting for the police to arrest Ralph, am alert for evidence of his villainy. This stress of waiting is taking its toll. I make an appointment and drive to the medical centre, and sit with a magazine in the waiting room, ignoring the TV on the wall blasting chat shows into our ears, and patiently wait for my name to be called.

'Mrs Rickaby!' greets the young woman who I am to see. 'How are you today? What can I do for you?'

Already the doctor has looked at her wristwatch twice. I've barely had time to sit down and clear my throat.

'A little stiffness…in my left ankle…' I begin.

She wraps the blood pressure cuff around my arm and pumps. 'All good here,' she reports gleefully. 'Are you on any medication?' she asks, looking at my details on her computer screen.

'No…'

'Last blood tests a year ago…better do those…'

'It's my ankle…'

The doctor prints out the pathology request and invites me to climb onto the examination table. She pokes and prods and manipulates my ankle, compares it to the other. 'A sprain, you say? Looks all right now. Perhaps a little arthritis gel? You're doing that? I'll see you to review in a week or so after your blood test,' she says. 'Just get a little exercise. Walking is the best…'

I thank her and leave, wondering why I bothered. Shivering, I throw the pathology request into the rubbish bin as I leave the surgery. They can make a pincushion out of somebody else.

I mustn't cry. I really mustn't. I am too old to cry.

Yet I can feel the telltale ache in the soft lining of my mouth, the taste of tears in my saliva. I am shivering with cold as I leave the medical centre. Happy thought: think of a happy thought. But what?

I am walking out of the medical centre into the street. I rummage in my handbag for sunglasses. Down the street there is a sidewalk café. Tables in the sun, so I can leave my glasses on for camouflage. I sit down and order cappuccino and chocolate cake. Yes, I know it is bad for me, but sometimes dense, rich chocolate is the only available comfort. I use the white paper napkin to wipe the corner of my eye. For some reason, I cannot find any tissues, not even a used one, in my bag.

Auntie Mabel was big on handkerchiefs. Always a lace-edged one tucked into her sleeve. If she asked me if I had a fresh one as I left the house each day, she felt that she was doing her duty. Poor Auntie Mabel, what a little life she had. She was my great aunt really. My father's spinster aunt, his only living relative. And poor me.

The coffee is good, the sun warm on my neck. I begin to calm down. I close my eyes and rest a little, think of nothing but the heat on my skin. I form a smile with my unwilling lips. They say this works. Fake it until you make it. Feels like I have been faking it my whole life.

A man and his blonde Labrador guide dog walk up and take a table nearby. The dog, quiet and obedient, lies beneath the table. One of the café staff brings out a bowl of water for the animal. The man orders cappuccino. He also wears dark glasses. I admire the composure of man and dog. Wish for it, would trade my eyes…?

No. The colours of the world, too vivid to lose. Too important to a painter. What's a few cleansing tears?

*

'What do you think about?' my mother had asked one day as we were packing for yet another swimming event. 'What goes through your mind on these long swims?'

Think about? How to explain the swirling non-verbal currents of sensation and emotion, memory and survival instinct that engulfed me each time I immersed myself in the unforgiving sea? How I kept reminding myself, frozen by icy seas and parched by salt, to breathe in and out, how I measured each moment in the frigid water by counting out the rhythm of my strokes, the number of my kicks. The tempo of the swell, rising and falling, the rhythm of the ocean, inviting me to dance. The disorienting haze of grey-green water through foggy goggles. Breathing as if through a saturated blanket. Struggling for sounds and direction, hoping to sense vibrations in the water like a fish. The supernatural energy of swimming through raging seas, totally immersed in the dramatic power of nature. The struggle to keep heat in my body as the cold waves sucked it from my skin. The sense of being connected to something larger than myself, in another sphere, as if I had learned to fly. Surviving each second and beginning another; stringing the seconds of endurance into minutes of movement; massing the minutes into the mountainous hours that carried me to the finish, the indistinct shoreline and my parents.

'I think about finishing,' I say. 'I think about making you and Dad proud.'

I couldn't really tell my other thoughts, the thoughts about the boy who didn't swim back. At fourteen, Dimitri and I were the youngest in the training squad. He had casual, dark-haired good looks and the body of an athlete. I was a dumpy girl, not built like an Amazonian sportswoman archetype at all. Teachers were always surprised at my parents' letters requesting time away from school for swim meets: I didn't have the appearance of an athlete and I certainly never distinguished myself on the sporting field. My attributes were to do with buoyancy, stamina and endurance: these things were not obvious to others when I was out of the water.

Dimitri could have been a sprinter. He was on the relay team and won individual races. But something about long swims in the ocean seduced him: like me, he preferred the open sea to chlorine-saturated pools. This common preference drew us together. Like me, he was an only child. A dreamy boy, he borrowed my books and talked of faraway places. He thought that swimming would take him around the world. We became training buddies and often travelled to competitions in the back of my dad's Holden. This led to a bit of teasing from other swimmers.

'Where's your girlfriend?' the relay team would jibe. 'Getting married soon?'

Dimitri had enough sense to take no notice. We were easy in each other's company. There was no awkwardness or silliness in our friendship. In many ways, he was a stand-in brother and would bring me little gifts: a banksia leaf, serrated like a saw; a pebble, streaked with lines of white; the first wild-grown freesia of spring.

One day, though, I could see as we left for a competition that he was rattled. He was running late, dived straight into my dad's car with his towel falling out of his duffel bag, his shirt unbuttoned and his shoes unlaced.

My father, annoyed, drove in silence after a curt 'Hello, lad. Sleep in?'

Dmitri gave me an apologetic glance, but spent the entire trip in silence, staring out the side window. Engrossed in a romantic novel, I paid little attention. Reading in the car never made me sick.

Once we arrived at the competition, we did our usual warm-ups, changed into our gear, lathered ourselves in lanolin. It was a river swim, one we had done before. Across the wide mouth of the river, ending where the water swelled into a round lagoon before entering the sea.

I hugged Dimitri for good luck, as I often did. Something in his tight shoulders made me stand back and look searchingly into his dark eyes: but he walked away, shaking his long limbs, limbering up. That was the last time I ever hugged him.

They pulled his lifeless body from the lagoon late that evening. No one had seen him leave the pack of swimmers, digress from the route and head for the sea. He was snagged in a net below the bridge that spanned the lagoon. It was not something that should have happened.

It was not something my parents ever discussed. Dimitri's parents moved away soon after. There was no grief counselling in those days. It was a time of stoicism, discreet silence and stiff upper lips. The suggestion that Dimitri, an experienced swimmer, had purposefully drowned could not be admitted or examined. The relay team found another swimmer; I carried on training, alone.

*

It seems to me that most people have a best friend through their schooldays. I seemed to have fallen off that agenda. I mixed vaguely with the sporty girls at high school, sat in the vicinity of their golden aura at lunch, but when birthday invitations and other events arrived, I was usually tied up with swimming commitments. Training took priority over visits to friend's houses or group gossips at the local milk bar. I held myself aloof and, after a while, nobody bothered with me.

At secretarial school, in those dark days after Mum and Dad died, I met a couple of keen trainee stenographers who took me under their wing. Slightly older and more worldly-wise, this pair were attendants at my wedding, looked after all the details of choosing flowers, dresses, advised on the cake. I think they hoped that some of the wedding luck would rub off on them and their lack-lustre love lives. Aunt Mabel encouraged their involvement, although she put her foot down about alcohol, and we had a teetotal reception in the local hall.

I lost touch with those friends when Howard and I moved to the country. There were other couples to socialise with, other parents when the children came along. No one close, though, until Jennifer, my painting mentor took me under her wing. I met her first at a Country Womens' Association fair. Jennifer was set up under a marquee doing painting demonstrations, selling work to locals, offering lessons. Something about her calm talent attracted me; the gracious way she looped up her soft, dark hair into an Edwardian style so out of date it was modish; her easy way of showing how a line and a pigment could be married to form a harmonious picture.

'Trust yourself,' she had often said. 'It is only a painting, after all.'

Jennifer's studio was a converted milking shed. The open stalls had been glassed in: skylights installed, insulation placed between the galvanised-iron roofing and a false ceiling of knotted pine. It could be hot in summer, but Jennifer would open the louvre windows to catch a breeze; wickedly cold in winter, but there was a wood-burning stove that she kept stoked and roaring.

The cows were long gone: Jennifer's farmer husband Bill had sold land to developers, keeping just enough for his horses and agistment business. They also did riding holidays, with accommodation in the commodious weatherboard farmhouse and convict-built stables. Later they branched out into painting holidays and master classes for art students. I went along to these, as a kind of apprentice/helper, handing out paints and washing brushes.

Jennifer had exhibited widely in galleries and sold her work internationally. When I knew her, her eyes had begun to fail, and her work was becoming larger and more vibrant. She gave me cheap, one-on-one lessons during the week, and after a while she wouldn't take payment, except in kind. 'I owe you,' she had said. 'You help me out in so many other ways.' Having a local friend with similar interests meant a lot to her, I know: all her artist friends were far away in the city or overseas. I could just drop by and chat. When other artists did visit, often en masse for a weekend, the studio was full of shop talk, wine and rowdy discussions long into the night. I went once or twice, as invited, but then stayed away. I was never going to be one of their crowd.

Looking back now, I see that Jennifer taught me much more than oils and watercolours, line and composition. She also taught me how creativity helps us to live, survive and flourish. As her eyesight failed and her paintings became bigger, bolder and less constrained, Jennifer also entered a new phase of confidential conversation with me, talking about her past. Her home in Europe and her lost Jewish family; the struggles of war and famine, relocation and identity.

In some of the paintings during these later days, there was a recurring theme of a forest. Tall, slender, mostly branchless trunks, reaching in parallel splendour to a dark sky above; only at the very tops did the trees sprout branches and leaves, as if they reached for a far-off source of light. In a very stylised way, unusual for a painter whose bread and butter had been botanical realism, the paintings had a storybook quality, a magical sense of another world. I wouldn't have been surprised to find Cinderella's slipper or Red Riding's hood hidden beneath one of the exposed, arched tree roots.

One day, emboldened by her candour, I had asked Jennifer what these paintings meant, and where she was finding her inspiration.

'The circle is closing,' she had said softly. 'The end is the beginning… and the beginning is the end. I see my childhood imaginings returning. I step back to dreams of my homeland, the forests of my father's stories. I'm painting from my mind's eye.' Her cloudy brown eyes looked kindly at my puzzled face. 'One day you'll know this,' she said with a reassuring pat to my forearm. 'Now, will you kindly put on the kettle for some tea?'

It took me years of pondering Jennifer's words to understand that painting is not just a means of making a living, although it can be that. It is not about calming our psyches or even marking time in this world; it is a way of understanding, an essential tool for the journey, a never-finished map that leads us home.

*

The strains of music coming from my radio change: after a pause following the final chord of Beethoven's symphony, something softer and gentler has begun: I step out of the shower to listen more closely. Yes, that familiar melody… It is an orchestral version of *Wiegenlied*. Dignified, unhurried, and with a solo cello that is almost like a human voice. It soothes and calms, exhorts one to tranquillity. The answering violins trill down lazily, a lingering echo of the soothing tune. Flutes take up the motif. I am immersed and cleansed by the sound. As the piece finishes, I switch off the radio. I don't want the chatter of the announcer to interfere with my musical memories. I step back into the running shower, humming slowly, rotating beneath the warm spray. Tum, tum, tum ta-da-da-dah – Tum, tum, tum ta-da-da-dah – de-dum-dum-de-dum-da-da – de-dum-da-de-dum-da-dah – I could almost be in the ocean, kicking and floating through the waves.

*

Sometimes when I wake in the night, I think I am wrapped in Mum's old green satin eiderdown, lying on the back seat of Dad's car, on the way home from a swimming race. If I don't open my eyes, I can see the brilliant stars of a country sky through the car window, the crescent moon lighting our travels. It is peaceful, quiet, serene…then the sudden swerve and jolt of impact, the hot memory of pain and loss. It is no use rolling over and looking for sleep after these nightmares. I have to rise from my bed, wrap myself in a dressing gown and go sensibly to the kitchen, make myself tea, and possibly toast. I take this back to bed and make myself physically comfortable. I take up the Scottish author's latest book so that his calm voice will soothe me. I turn on the radio low; there are programs for insomniacs playing suitable tunes at all hours. Missy isn't bothered by my night-time prowling. She slumbers on.

*

It is quite amazing to me how easily habits, both good ones and bad, are formed. The single glass of Chardonnay in the evening can easily become a bottle, and then two; one spoon of tiramisu becomes a bowlful; an attentive man becomes a lover to a lonely woman, then her husband, whether or not she wanted or needed one, in her rational mind. But loneliness does odd things to one, and even the simplest of pleasures can become a habit, a need, a necessity.

Every morning now, about ten, I drive to the aquatic centre, put on my modest navy blue swimsuit, cover my hair and sensitive ears with a white bathing cap, and dive into clear, clean water and swim up and down like a beetle for an hour. (I found the goggles irritating and discarded them after the first session.) An hour isn't much when you have swum long distance, raced in all weathers and conquered the English Channel: but all that is long ago, and I am old now, older than I care to admit, but my body remembers the physical demands I once made of it, falls easily into the rhythm of breath, stroke, kick, so my mind has nothing to do except float along for the ride, and remember where my towel is at the end of the hour.

There is a clock high on the mosaic-tiled wall, which I check on a turn to see if my hour is up. But today, it is the harsh voice of a schoolteacher shouting instructions as she herds a class of primary school children into the pool area for swimming lessons that arouses me to consciousness and indicates it is time to leave.

My towel is on a bench at the opposite end of the pool – I break my Australian crawl rhythm and breaststroke quietly down towards it. A child, aged about six or seven, runs and leaps and bombs into the water, landing on my white-capped head. Winded, but not concussed, I am dragged from the pool by the swimming teacher and am about to be given mouth-to-mouth by her when I manage to roll over and vomit instead, putting paid to that little activity.

The teacher is so sorry, the aquatic centre staff concerned, first aid person called, ambulance suggested, but 'NO, NO, NO,' I insist. I accept a complimentary coffee in the café and allow them to monitor my vital signs for twenty minutes. Then I drive sedately home, wishing that my quiet life of painting and orchid growing had never been disturbed by any whiff of romance, wedding news or need to change.

Needless to say, I have a raging headache and am in no mood for conversation, do not hurry to answer, but let the ringing phone go to the message machine as I walk into my villa. Almost immediately, I regret this. Pouring myself a glass of water and searching in in the cupboard for paracetamol, I hear the voice of my daughter Susan say, 'Mum, it's Susan. Sorry to miss you… Have you seen the news? Don't worry, I'm perfectly OK. I'm coming home…expect me on the tenth…

can you fetch me from the airport? How is the police investigation progressing? Has Ralph been arrested? I'll need to stay with you for a couple of months…you don't mind, do you? It'll be fun to be together again! Dying to meet my sister-in-law–to-be! Love you! See you soon! Will call you on your mobile as soon as we land – you have got it charged up, haven't you? Bye!'

*

I love my daughter dearly, I really do, but at times I wish she were less impulsive. This sudden leaving of Madrid has me all in a spin. Is she all right? Did something go wrong? Is she ill? A bad love affair? An accident? No, it is me who has had the accident, my head is pounding and my neck aches as if a small elephant has perched on my shoulders and is leaning against my head demanding piggybacks. I will call Susan tomorrow, I really will, but right now I must take a steaming hot shower, paracetamol or something stronger if I can find the leftover tablets from last year's painful wrist sprain, and go to bed, even though it is barely midday.

Missy is sympathetic, and after eating the remains of her breakfast, comes companionably to bed. I lie propped on my pillows with a heat pack listening to Mozart. I cannot read, or think, or sleep. Perhaps I am in shock. Might visit the doctor tomorrow after all.

I lie awake during the afternoon, listening to a full concerto, and then the soothing tones of the radio announcer is replaced by a sharp nasal voice belonging to a newsreader who says there is a wave of terrorist attacks in Europe, and Australians are advised not to travel. A train has been bombed in Madrid (oh, Susan!) with many dead and heavy casualties. An influx of returning nationals is expected, and the air force is sending extra planes.

'Howard,' I cry to the lifeless picture on the wall. 'I wish you were here.' I am not one of those widows who talk to their lost loved ones, kiss pictures, sense presences or commemorate anniversaries of important dates. But sometimes, just sometimes, the perpetual sad ache of loss wells up into a torrent of need, and this is one of those times. If it weren't bad enough, worrying about Irene, being on perpetual alert for Ralph's sinister intent, and waiting for the police to nab him – I don't know how much more stress I can take.

I reach out for Missy, weep into her white fur, and worry about the state of the world.

*

I did sleep after that, must have been exhaustion and pills. I wake with the dull sense of being out of synch at 6 p.m., let Missy out for some air and turn on the TV for the evening news. Mesmerised, I watch the same story on three channels, one after the other, all reporting in dramatic tones the senseless and tragic loss of innocent life. Missy comes back inside and sits with me on the sofa, looking at me with her intense blue eyes. It is if she is urging me to action. A second cup of tea and a slice of fruit cake provide a hit of energy. It is then that I realise I must get moving and organise myself to drive to Sydney to meet Susan. I must make arrangements.

I call Annette first and ask her to look after Missy, because I don't know exactly when Susan is arriving, and I might be gone a day or two.

'Only too happy to help,' Annette says. 'I'm as free as a bird. The doctor has given me the all-clear and I would love to look after Missy.'

'That is great news, Annette! So glad you're OK.'

'Yes. I admit I was worried. I've been watching the news. Dreadful, dreadful times… Hope your daughter's OK…'

'She's fine,' I say, desperately wanting this to be so, believing it to be so, praying it is so. 'You are marvellous, Annette. I am grateful for your help with Missy. I'll be back as soon as I can.'

'I'll keep an eye on Ralph and Irene too,' Annette says. 'Still no news from the police? I can't believe it's taking so long for something to happen. Perhaps we should…'

'We simply have to wait,' I say firmly. I have no energy left to plot with Annette.

I find the mobile phone and charge it up – I get tired of doing this when I use it so seldom, have no reason to carry it around with me. I pack an overnight bag, have another piece of fruit cake, and finally go to bed and sleep like a log until dawn.

I am not a bad driver, and I am not a good driver. I am like most people I know, careful and yet forgetful, competent to drive around quiet suburban streets and less successful on busy, unfamiliar main roads and highways. Since I wake early, I get ready, feed Missy (Annette will be over later to look in on her) have a cup of tea and get into the car, driving south in the pearly morning light.

Everything is going well, I am making good time, so I stop at a café and have a late breakfast of raisin toast and coffee, buy a banana for a snack later on. There aren't many other customers, just a few truckies eating large fried breakfasts, some smoking outside in the car park.

I get back behind the wheel and reverse out, at the same time adjusting the radio to my favourite classical station, because somehow it has been jolted off the setting. This is my mistake. I should be paying more attention, don't see the dog running along behind the row of cars, ready to leap into the plumber's ute parked nearby.

I hear a sickening crunch of bone as the car rolls over something lumpy and unexpected.

No one could be sorrier than I am about the poor dog crushed beneath my wheel. The plumber is shouting and cursing, threatening and waving his arms at me. A crowd gathers, a police car arrives, a policewoman takes me inside for another cup of coffee. At last the fuss subsides, people get into their vehicles and drive away, the plumber gives his details to the police and I give mine, but I am made to understand that there will be no legal consequences. Through the policewoman, I offer the plumber money, for vet expenses, a new puppy, whatever – it is disdainfully rejected. I couldn't feel more crushed. (Oh, Howard! I know what Irene means about having someone of your own. I think about calling Mike, but no, I should stand on my own two feet.)

I have a third coffee, by myself, visit the ladies room and then depart, laden with caffeine, trying to maintain an acceptable speed, not too fast, not too slow, all the way down to the city. I don't stop again. I drive right into the heart of town, over the harbour bridge and through tunnels, until I reach the airport hotel. I book in and fall asleep on the large, flat, quilted bed cover, mobile phone within reach for when Susan calls.

It is a long time before the plane arrives. Calmer now, and trying to forget about the poor dog, I have the strange luxury of being alone in the hotel with nothing to do. I watch a little TV: but that doesn't feel right without Missy on my lap. I wander downstairs and browse the very expensive gift shops and boutiques. I have afternoon tea in the lounge: Earl Grey and small sandwiches, petit fours. I buy a paperback novel and retreat upstairs, snuggle into bed and read. I allow myself a small bottle of wine from the minibar, and some peanuts, idling as though I have all the time in the world. I am longing to be home: I can't find my classical station on the bedside radio.

I doze in the afternoon and wake around 8 pm. I order an omelette from room service, although I am not hungry. I wish Susan would arrive. All this hanging around, worrying and snacking will undo all the good my swimming has achieved.

At last she phones around midnight: the plane has landed.

When she arrives at the door, she is grey-faced and dishevelled. I run a hot bath and lead her to it; bring her hot tea that she drinks while soaking. She tells me a little of the drama: assures me she is unhurt. I don't push her but wait until she is ready to talk.

Eventually she finds the words. 'We were on the train that was hit,' Susan says. 'Marco and I. Travelling back into the city after a weekend away. In the last carriage. It was the front of the train that carried the bomb. We were tossed around, flung out of our seats…Marco's head was grazed by a shattered window – he protected me with his body – but apart from that, we were just shaken up. It was horrible, like a war zone. Body parts and blood, twisted metal, shards of glass… We climbed out of the carriage, it was tipped on one side, and walked in the dark along the railway track towards the lights of the rescue teams. Mum, I never want to experience anything like that ever again.'

I wash her hair for her, gently massaging her scalp with lemon-scented foam and rinsing the shampoo off with fresh water, shielding her eyes with one hand laid across her forehead as I had done when she was little. It is a moment of reconnection, a tenderness we have not shared for many years.

After the bath, she declares she is ravenous, so despite the early hour, we order full English breakfasts from room service. She eats, wrapped in a white towelling robe, propped in one of the beds. We talk more, and then she nods off to sleep. I lie on the other bed and read my novel, glancing up every now and then just to look at her. I have not watched my daughter sleeping since she was a small child. She is older, of course, than when I last saw her, slightly grey at her temples (my daughter!) but still lithe and youthful in her figure, physically unharmed. Sleeping, she looks very young in the face, the worry lines on her forehead have smoothed out and her lips relaxed. She is all right, nothing that some rest won't cure. I am relieved and reassured, so happy to have her home in her own country again.

She has been away so long. At the end of her fine arts degree, Susan won a scholarship for further study in London. After that, she progressed to various jobs and assignments in Europe, only coming home briefly for quick visits. The longest of them was for her father's funeral. Howard and Susan had been very close, even after she left home, calling often and keeping in touch. She would tell me, breathlessly, of her current boyfriend and the excitements of new places and towns; exactly what she discussed with her father I do not know, but a conversation with his daughter always left Howard with a sparkle in his eye and a quickness in his step. When he died, Susan felt it keenly, especially since she had expected that there would be plenty of years ahead to return home and be with us in our old age. Howard's death is, I think, one of the reasons she has stayed away so long: to see me in a life without him must drive home the loss more keenly, make it more final.

Susan sleeps for ten hours. I read my novel and doze, just wait for her to wake. We decide to visit the day spa in the hotel, have various treatments and massages to lighten our spirits. Susan has her hair cut and restyled; I enjoy a pedicure and back massage. Feeling much refreshed, we book a table in the restaurant for a welcome home dinner.

Sitting at the white linen-covered table, watching the other diners arrive, Susan calls Mike and discusses the situation in Madrid. The waiter brings us champagne flutes of pink bubbles; I nibble on some olives and pâté. More people are coming in now: quite a number are gathered at the adjoining bar. I catch a glimpse of a familiar head: the tossing, dark locks too distinctive to mistake.

Susan finishes her conversation and lays her phone on the table. 'You look like you've seen a ghost!'

'Not a ghost, a demon in disguise,' I say.

'Who?'

'Don't look round,' I instruct, 'but when you can, notice the dark-haired woman in the wrap-around frock, standing at the bar.'

'Why? Who is she?'

'Rachel. Ralph's supposed cousin. You know, the man hoodwinking my neighbour Irene.'

Susan slides her arm across the table, knocking her phone to the floor. She leans over to pick it up and, as she scoops it in her hand, she swivels round to observe the bar. In a swift motion, she raises the phone and takes a photo of Rachel standing with her arms draped around the neck of a suited businessman, who sits, wide-legged, on a bar stool.

'Why did you do that?'

'I thought the man might be your Ralph.'

'Not *my* Ralph, and no, not him.'

'At any rate,' says Susan, 'cousin or not, that woman is a high-class hooker.'

I looked across at the group of businessmen at the bar. There were two women, Rachel and one other high-heeled, highly made-up bottle blonde. Both of them were showing a great deal of leg and even more cleavage. Susan is right.

'So, my little brother is getting married,' Susan remarks.

'Yes! You'll like Elise,' I say. 'She and Mike just look right together. Although I've only met her twice! Things have moved so fast.'

'Strange to think of Mike as a grown-up man with a family.'

'Yes, I think that's on the cards. Some little nieces or nephews for you, sooner or later.'

'We're all getting old,' says Susan.

'Speak for yourself!'

'I am.'

The silent waiter comes by and expertly fills our water glasses. The restaurant is emptying, but having slept most of the day, Susan is in no rush to turn in.

'Mum, I think I'm home for good,' says Susan, tasting a small spoonful of the tiramisu we are sharing.

'That's wonderful!' I don't try to hide my pleasure at this news. 'Because of the problems in Madrid? Or some other reason?'

'Well…I've been thinking for a while that it's time to come home. To look after you in your dotage.'

'I don't need looking after.'

'Joking!' Susan raises both palms in a pose of surrender. 'But I do want to be here,' she says. 'If you ever need me.'

'What about Marco?' I ask quietly, taking a little more tiramisu. Marco is her current bloke. From what I can gather, they have an easy-come, easy-go, type of relationship.

'He's getting married.'

'What?'

'Getting married to a third cousin. After the bomb, as we were waiting in a first aid centre to be checked over, he told me all about it, said he needed to stop wasting time with me and marry the girl his family has picked for him. Apparently, it's been arranged since they were babies.'

I lay down my spoon, reach out my hand to cover hers.

'Nothing like a disaster to show people what's really important to them,' she winced. 'Bastard. But it's all right. He was never the love of my life,' Susan states with a sigh.

'What will you do?' I ask.

'I've severed all my ties and brought home all my goods and chattels,' she replies. 'Whatever I've forgotten, Marco and his bride can keep in remembrance of me. Seems like there could be some job openings in Canberra soon… If I'm lucky, I might grab one of those, try living in the capital.'

'It'll be a bit different to Madrid.'

'I've had my fill of bullfights and paella. And Latin lovers.'

The waiter is standing nearby like a silent guardsman, getting impatient, so we finish up and leave the restaurant arm in arm. We chat easily as we head back to the room, pack our things, and plan for an early trip home tomorrow. Susan is talkative about job possibilities and where she might settle.

'I'm so glad you're home to stay,' I say, as we turn out the bedside lights.

'Me too.'

6

Impromptu

Susan and I arrive home laden with her many boxes and bundles. I stagger from the car and immediately Annette is there too, red in the face and out of breath.

'Saw you drive up,' she says. 'I'm most dreadfully sorry.'

'Sorry about what?' I ask.

'It's Missy. She's at the vet. Poison. I don't know HOW it happened. I'm most dreadfully sorry. The police say…'

'Police?'

'Yes, that's the other thing…you were burgled last night. Made quite a mess. They think the burglar put poison in Missy's bowl. But why would a thief take the time to do such a thing? Unless it was…' Annette shot a swift look at Susan, not sure what to say in front of my daughter. '…Ralph…' she mouths silently behind Susan's back. 'I'm so dreadfully sorry,' she goes on, aloud. 'That such a thing should have happened on my watch, so to speak. I blame myself for not taking Missy home to my house.'

I go in and survey the living room. I sit on a dining room chair, my feet surrounded by broken stems of orchid, spilled potting mix and shards of terrarium glass. The house is a mess, but at first glance I can't see anything missing.

'The vet says Missy will recover,' says Annette. 'Apparently I found her just in time.'

Susan is outside at the car.

'I don't think it was Ralph,' I say.

Vision of the angry plumber plays like a news reel in my head, his

gesturing and threatening words, over and over. He knew my name
and address. He couldn't have, could he?

*

Susan, my amazingly confident adult daughter, walks into the
dishevelled house and takes charge of the situation. A full head taller
than me, and built with the same lithe limbs her father had, her
gestures mirror Howards's so exactly, that I am filled with longing for
him, from my lips to my tingling finger tips.

'Have the police been?' she asks.

'Yes, took photos and made notes. Said we could clean up,' replies
Annette.

I walk across my living room floor, crunching broken glass, splatters
of watercolour pigment and torn orchid petals in to the pale sisal carpet.
Whoever made his mess was malicious – the tubes of paint have been
opened, the lids tossed aside, and large feet have stomped the tubes to
send paint squirting in obscene lines and splodges over the floor. There
is a strong odour of alcohol. The spare room looks untouched, so we put
Susan's luggage in there. My bedroom is splattered with magenta paint
– why would anyone bother? And someone has relieved themselves in
the middle of my bed. My radio has been smashed against the wall. I
check my jewellery, my small stash of cash and documents…only some
money has been taken.

'What the police couldn't work out,' continues Annette, 'is how the
thieves got in. Asked if you'd lost a key recently. There was no damage
to any window or door, the door was found open, unlocked…'

I think back to when I left for Sydney, admitting to myself that I
was not in top form that day, after the swimming pool episode. Maybe I
didn't lock up properly? But no, I remember clearly locking up, leaving
Missy in the laundry to wait for Annette's visit, locking the French
doors and pulling the curtains closed. Those curtains have been pulled
from their track and now lie shredded on the ground. No one else has
a key. I gave Annette my other spare. No one else…except Irene.

The last time I wore this black suit was at Howard's funeral. It wasn't new then: I had bought it for a wedding we were invited to, the bride a stranger to me, but the daughter of a work colleague of Howard's. It used not to be the thing to wear black to weddings; but now everyone wears black all the time, according to Susan. I don't; if buying trousers I'd rather choose navy, which is just as smart, and doesn't get that washed-out greyed look so soon that black trousers get when not laundered well. I haven't worn this suit except on those two occasions: but in a wardrobe purge, it always gets put back on the rail in its dry cleaner's plastic wrapping, it is so suitable for the odd wedding or funeral, and the brass buttons and Chanel piping still look classic and smart, although the bouclé fabric is out of date.

I reach into the bottom of the wardrobe for my black court shoes, carefully boxed to protect them from dust and mould. I know I have a new pair of sheer black pantyhose in my drawer somewhere. I will look presentable at poor Larry's funeral, not let the side down.

There have been three deaths and three funerals in the village this week. Two were very elderly, unwell women in their nineties, from the nursing home, who I did not know at all. I did not attend their services, felt no need to make any gesture.

(Annette went to both: she goes to every funeral, attends every meeting. It all falls under her motto of 'keeping busy'. Also, a way of making sure someone will attend her own funeral, I suspect. But what does it matter? How will anyone know who attends their own funeral? I don't think we will be up on a cloud watching. But perhaps I am wrong.)

No, I didn't know either of those women at all, but Larry is different. Larry was a foundation member of the Orchid Society. Together with his wife Joan, the most knowledgeable and reasonable couple of the group, a joy to know. Larry was a gentleman in every respect, a guru in horticultural circles and a generous neighbour. We will miss him tremendously. Poor Joan. Another widow in this community full of ageing women. We will gather round her and do our best. Annette has already been a daily visitor since Joan found Larry dead on the garage floor, putting away his clubs after a day of golf. But the family have arrived now, the son and two daughters, with their spouses and children, so the neighbours take a step back to allow the family to grieve. That is how things are done. When the family go, we will take turns at popping in, offering little outings, shopping help, a friendly phone call. We will not intrude but stand ready to stand beside. And there will be a good turnout at the funeral. We shall do them proud.

'Is that what you're wearing?' asks Susan. 'Do you want me to come?'

'You don't need to come,' I reply. 'Isn't this suit all right?'

'Yes, very classic. You've lost weight, haven't you? Are you sick?'

'No, just exercise. I've been swimming every day,' I admit. 'Until you arrived.'

'OH! Sorry! Did I disrupt your routine?'

'Doesn't matter. Doesn't matter at all. Maybe we can both go tomorrow.'

'Yeah, OK. I'll do a grocery shop today if you like. While you're out?'

'If you like… My list is near the phone. Is that Annette at the door already?'

Susan lets Annette in and I do up my buttons, step into my shoes, pick up my handbag. As we leave, Susan hugs me for a moment longer than is usual, and I know we are both remembering the day of Howard's funeral. I slip on sunglasses as I step outside. The day is sunny and windy, and there is already something in my eye. Annette has her little car ready to drive us to the chapel. I know that while I am gone, Susan will console herself by being very efficient with the shopping, and the last of the tidying up after the burglary. We are all keeping busy, every day, in our own way.

*

'That isn't really Mozart, you know. It's by someone else.' Irene jabs the lid of the little walnut music box Susan has brought me from Europe. It is playing *Wiegenlied.*

'I don't really mind who wrote it.' My memories of the piece are about my mother: the composer is immaterial.

'I thought you were all for truth and transparency.'

'Concerning a two-hundred-year-old melody? I hardly think it matters, except to the music historian.'

'Such a sentimental tune…'

I close the music box lid abruptly. I do not wish for my comfortable associations to be tainted with Irene's cynicism. If I cannot be a little sentimental about a song my mother once played, then what comfort is left in the world?

Irene and Ralph have come over for drinks and nibbles. Susan wanted to get a first-hand look at Ralph and size up the situation for herself. I observed him closely, as he walked over my recently cleaned living room, for any sense of guilt in his eyes or interest in our clean-up of the vandalism to my home. He gave nothing away. Out in the courtyard, Susan has him engaged in conversation about travel. Places in Spain they have both seen and enjoyed. Irene is a little put out to be left inside with me. I go to the kitchen and pull some hot canapés from the oven. I pass Irene a handful of napkins and we go out to join them. Missy has made herself scarce.

'I'm sure I was a bullfighter in another life,' declares Ralph, shaking the red table napkin at Irene with a dramatic flourish. 'The spectacle! The excitement…the blood!'

'O-leh!' cries Irene, getting into the mood.

'Poor bulls,' I say. 'Just innocent animals used for sport.'

'Have you been to Spain, Eileen?' Ralph asks.

'No,' I reply. 'Other parts of Europe, but not Spain. I probably would have visited Susan there, if she'd stayed, but…'

'Or not,' says Susan. 'Mum, you never once talked about visiting.'

'Now we'll never know,' I say, handing around prawn toasts. 'Have one of these, Ralph. Quite tasty.'

'We should be watching our waistlines,' simpers Irene. 'For the wedding.'

'Plenty of exercise opportunities to work off the calories!' says Ralph with a leer.

'Have you got your outfits organised?' asks Susan, steering the conversation onto commonplace wedding talk.

We linger in the courtyard until the twilight darkens to a moonless night. Irene and Ralph take their leave.

As we clear up the kitchen together, Susan says pointedly, 'He's a complete con artist. I'll tell you one thing, Mum, that man has *never* been to Spain.'

*

Although there are still a couple of stubborn stains on the carpet, most of the burglary damage has been put to rights. Susan has been working like a demon, washing and repainting walls. Curtains have been replaced, broken items tossed away. I ordered more art supplies online: I am particular about the quality of my pigments and brushes. Despite attempts to clean my fouled bed, the smell lingered, so there was nothing for it but to buy a new one. It is now installed in my freshly painted room, complete with new doona and matching sheets, a whole new look.

Missy is unimpressed, is hesitant about the unfamiliar smells, wary of any change. I think she blames Susan for the upheaval, will not have a bar of her. The vet says Missy has recovered completely. I spoil her with treats, let her sleep all day on the sofa if she wants to, undisturbed. I feel so guilty, about both Missy and that poor plumber's dog. Perhaps I am unfit to have a pet. I open a tin of sardines, and Missy finishes the lot, sits down at the front door to give her face a comprehensive wash.

I walk into my bedroom. Is it my imagination, or can I still smell that foul odour? I open the windows wide, turn on the ceiling fan full blast. I search my cupboard for an unopened gift, I just know there is a little oil burner and assortment of essential oils I have never used… Ah, yes, here it is. I pour drops of citrus and lavender, light the burner.

'What are you doing?' asks Susan, leaning in the doorway.

'Just trying to get rid of the last of the smell.'

'It doesn't smell, Mother! It's just impossible. I've completely sanitised everything. All the bedding is new…'

'I know. But…'

'There is NO SMELL at ALL!' Susan retorts.

'Cats smell more keenly than we do. Missy won't come anywhere near the bedroom,' I say.

'Good thing too,' says my daughter. 'You let that cat sleep anywhere. Can't be healthy, letting her sleep on your bed.'

'Missy is very clean. She never goes beyond the courtyard. And she sees the vet regularly,' I say, adding more oil to the burner. 'She's cleaner than you or I.'

Susan stomps off and gets ready to play a round of golf. She goes off in a huff to meet Joan. I never knew that she had learnt to play golf, until she and Joan discussed it. Susan must have played in Europe – but there are many things I don't know about my daughter.

During our argument, Missy has been hiding under the sofa. I coax her out. She really isn't herself… I wonder if the poisoning has left any lasting damage. I never should have left her. Things have gone completely awry this year – ever since Irene introduced Ralph into our lives. I am so angry, I could –

I don't know what I could do. I cuddle Missy, stroke her. She doesn't purr. She hasn't purred since coming home from the vet.

*

Next morning, the phone rings. An unfamiliar voice asks for my daughter.

'Susan!' I call. 'Phone!'

Susan comes in from the courtyard, brushing soil from her hands. Ever busy, she has been weeding.

I go to my bedroom to plug in the new radio at my bedside, try to tune in my classical station. I have missed the soothing familiarity of it, these nights since the burglary.

'Can I borrow your car?' asks Susan, coming in the doorway. 'I have a job interview tomorrow in Canberra.'

My daughter is an art historian and conservator, and I know that jobs are hard to find in this speciality. I knew she would be moving to a city somewhere, am glad of this opportunity in her own country, yet have become used to her company already in this short time we have been together.

'Or should I rent one? I can do that, if you prefer,' Susan offers.

'No, no, don't be silly, take my car.'

'Are you sure? I'll only be gone a day or two. This opportunity has just come up, and I think I should grab it.'

'Definitely, you must, take my car. I won't need it. The shopping's all done.'

'OK.' Susan goes back to the phone to arrange the details.

Then a whirl of packing and goodbyes. My daughter does nothing slowly or hesitantly. Suddenly the door closes, and she is gone. Missy jumps onto my lap. We sit together, my hand stroking her head, her purring warmth heavy on my lap.

'Back to normal, for a little while, Missy,' I say.

As the light fades, I have a scratch meal of cheese on toast, a long scented bath. I decide to settle in for an early night in my new bed, listening to the radio and reading my favourite Scottish author. Missy decides to try out the bed and jumps up, circles round and round.

The fresh new sheets must smell suspicious, although Susan has laundered them before we made up the bed. I know it pleased Susan to do it: she felt useful and needed, advising me about the purchases, colours, revamping my room, making the vandalism of my home an opportunity for pleasure, rather than a nuisance, a threat.

The room does look good. But it lacks the familiarity of my old quilt, the comfortable old colour scheme. I wonder if I will be able to sleep. Missy looks doubtful. It may take us some time to settle in the unfamiliar bedding, the smell of new paint and upholstery mixed with my essential oils.

I sit on the bed and bounce a little. Higher than the old bed, this one leaves my feet dangling in the air. Short legs. I have always had short legs. Unusual for a swimmer, perhaps. But it was my powerful shoulders, my natural buoyancy and endurance in cold water that gave me the edge. Some inherited stamina, stubbornness perhaps, that made me a champion. These days my shoulders, hidden by sleeves in all weathers, are less athletic. Like any seventy-year-old's, my upper arms are draped in crêpey, loose skin dotted with sunspots. I think about Irene's thinner arms, her height, the casual elegance with which she carries herself. Was that what attracted Ralph? No, it was her money, my evil self immediately replies. But they are a couple, I remind myself. He can't find her repulsive. The vision of cousin Rachel in the kitchen pops into my head. He isn't doing without, I tell myself. All these little business trips. Enough to keep any man happy.

Once again, I mull over what I might say to Irene, what warning I could give her. But in my heart, I know she will never believe me; she wants to believe in Ralph's fidelity, to revel in his love.

I get into bed. Missy wanders around me and at last settles in beside my hip. Ears alert, she is still watchful. I am perched in bed and feel as if I might roll off. There is no body-sized hollow in which to snuggle. I adjust my pillows, try to read. I fear it will be a long night.

*

Although some weeks pass when I hardly use my car, perversely, not to have it in the garage at the ready makes me miss it with irrational need. Until Susan comes back with the car, I am landlocked: cannot go out on a whim or drive to the pool. I must use up my pantry and fridge food (although there is plenty) and contain my activities to walking distance.

The trouble is, I have no work on the go to absorb me. I have no painting problem to keep me occupied, no choices to make about colour and tone, no difficult details to render in two dimensions. I pull out some watercolour papers, pencils and pigments, sort through my brushes. I really want the new supplies I have ordered online, but they are slow in arriving. I watch for the day-glow vest and white helmet of our post-girl, on her nippy motorbike. Friendly and chatty, she is a popular bearer of good tidings as she wheels her way around the curves of our village streets. I know that she has been in trouble from her boss for taking so long to make deliveries in our area, but she sees it as a public service, chatting to retired folk and delivering a friendly smile with their letters and parcels.

No sign of her yet this morning, so I go into the kitchen and make coffee. Irene hasn't come over to join me for ages. I miss the chat but feel overwhelmed by her self-centred wedding plans and anecdotes about Ralph, even when he isn't with us, so am content with my own company. I turn over the pages of an art journal as I sip my hot beverage, still listening for the post-girl.

At last I hear the revs of her bike, the skid of her front wheel on concrete paving. I go out and yes! My package has arrived, with a couple of bills, and a pale mauve envelope which looks like a card. I thank her and, as the day is warming up, offer her a glass of chilled water. (I know everyone else in the village does the same. If she accepted all offers of refreshment, she would be as bloated as a water balloon.) Of course, she declines and smiles as she waves and buzzes off down the street, I am the last house in this cul de sac.

I take my mail into the house and read the bills, open the box and check my order. Last of all I open the card, after checking that the name on the front was actually mine, because it isn't my birthday or any other general time of the year when one might expect to receive greetings. There is no sender information on the envelope. It is a card with a beach scene on the front and, inside, a short message from the plumber whose dog I had run over. Apologising for his anger, admitting that he should have had the dog restrained, wishing me well. As a postscript, he writes that he has given the RSPCA a donation in poor Dusty's name, inviting me to do the same. Touched, I feel that I most certainly will do as he suggests. I feel that my faith in humanity is a little restored. But this doesn't sound like someone who would have trashed my house. So, if the plumber didn't break in, who did?

*

For many months after my parents died, marooned in an inland town far from the sea, alone in Aunt Mabel's spare room, in that stretch of anchorless drifting on unfamiliar tides, moonlit or in pre-dawn gloom, I lay awake with my sorrow, unable to find the release of sleep. Tears all used up, I would toss and roll on Auntie's embroidered linen sheets (never before used; retrieved from her cedar glory box chest with a reluctant sigh on the night of my arrival) wondering if, beyond that wrenching spiral of rending hot metal and unbearable pain, my parents had found a place of calm oblivion? Of peace and comfort, or at least some kind of perpetual anaesthetic and absence of agony? As time passed, my memories of the accident, once vivid and cinematic, became confused. I thought I recalled my mother's brief scream: but I could have dreamt it in some moment of snatched, tortured slumber. I do remember my father's heavy, indescribable sigh at the moment of impact, as his body parted company with his soul. Such things cannot be spoken of aloud. They belong to the reminiscences of the night: these sleepless hours that plague us in bouts of recurring despair: these seasons of transition and mourning.

The local doctor suggested sleeping pills, but stoic Auntie was hesitant of all medications, and I was too wrapped in my grief to look for relief. It was the local clergyman, brought in to console, who kindly said, 'Are you sleeping?' and introduced me to the local bushwalking club, the tennis doubles played on the church courts, the weekly energetic dances stomped out on the wooden floor of the hall that speared splinters into each foot that had earlier surrendered pinching high heels to the pile tossed under the bench seats in the corner. I allowed myself to be shepherded into these activities, scarcely caring what I did and where I went: but it was my salvation, because intense physical activity was what my body required, and sleep came once again each night as I fell, exhausted, onto the scratchy linen.

The room I slept in had been Aunt Mabel's as a girl. When her mother had died, she had moved into the main bedroom of the house. She slept in the old iron-framed double bed she was born in for the rest of her life. On my first night, she had said, 'Your father used the sleep-out when he came to stay,' indicating the veranda enclosed with louvres. 'But I suppose a girl had better be inside. You can have my old room.'

It hadn't been redecorated since Mabel's girlhood; was full of her books. Poems by Robert Louis Stevenson, Henry Kendall; sad Victorian novels in which virtuous children suffered illnesses and prayed on their deathbeds, before being transported to a better world by glorious winged angels. Lying awake at night, I would be mesmerised by the patterns of the gilded letters on those book spines, lit by the street light shining through the ecru lace curtain.

I went to secretarial school. I graduated and took a series of temporary office jobs, before settling into the law firm where Howard, bless him, was a junior partner. I would get off the bus several stops early, and walk for miles home, to exhaust myself and ensure the night would be kind. I would offer to shop or do various errands for auntie, to walk as much as possible, to feel that steady rhythm of my soles on gravel, concrete, or red pounded earth.

When Howard died, I knew to work myself hard walking, cleaning, packing up our marital home. The business of downsizing kept the older me tired enough to fall into sleep most nights. Here in the village, I have my regular routes around the perimeter of the golf course, the village green, the rose garden. It is level walking, pleasant and safe; sometimes if I am troubled, I walk the circuit twice to really tire myself. In this way, and with my nightly routine of bubble bath, Mozart and Missy, I have conditioned myself to avoid the torment of sleeplessness. It works most of the time.

But, with all this worrying about Irene, I find the insomnia returning. Always waiting and hoping the police are about to pounce. I lie awake and listen for any disturbances in my neighbour's house, try to cast from my mind images from old movies in which the heroine is being strangled by her faithless husband. I fret about the lack of police action. I am jumpy about small noises, apt to double-check the locks on the doors at night. I keep the mobile phone charged and in my dressing gown pocket at night, my coat pocket during the day. My reserves of calm are tested to the utmost.

Missy sheds white hairs all over the house. I have never known her to moult this much before.

I break my resolve and phone Bob. 'We can't stand the strain any longer,' I plead.

'It's out of my hands, Eileen,' he protests. 'Federal police have taken over now. This is a man wanted in countries all over Asia.'

*

I keep walking. I double my daily exercise. As usual, I stop at the park bench on a small knoll overlooking the golf course. This is a favourite place of mine: sometimes I sit for a long time, watching the kookaburras or currawongs feeding on insects on the slopes below, or communing with the restless wagtails bouncing from fence post to fence post, and back again. I take a photo or two on my digital camera. It is an artist thing, to be always on the lookout for new subjects to paint.

Below me, the clubhouse nestles in a grove of mature trees. At the front, it is a modest colonial sandstone house, with sweeping wrought iron verandas and terracotta chimney stacks. At the back, the restaurant and function rooms have been added on in a sympathetic style, although massively out of proportion: lots of paned glass and conservatory-style rooms. I have painted the front of the house several times: the European planting of the garden ensures a changing vista. In spring, the beds of daffodils and vines of wisteria looping around the veranda give a pretty subject for watercolours; in autumn, the deciduous trees provide an opportunity to run riot with exaggerated scarlet and gold; the bare branches in winter give a melancholy mood against a pale sky; and in summer, before the heat scorches the foliage, lush greens provide a nice contrast to the mellow sandstone blocks of the main house. In fact, four of my efforts now hang in the clubhouse foyer, unoriginally titled *The Four Seasons*, with a conspicuous notice declaring 'local artist'.

Today, the peaceful scene seems incongruous. The serene afternoon masks a lurking danger in our midst. I watch the gossiping currawongs, and think about a study in black and white, but doubt my ability to capture the sense of movement and life. Solid sandstone is an easier subject and doesn't twitch or flap its wings as the mauve shadows of afternoon glide over its glowing face. Often there are other walkers who pause for a rest and a snatch of conversation on the bench. Larry was one of them, but he is gone now. I should drop by and see Joan, invite her to walk with me. I know how much exercise is needed in times of mourning. It would be nice, I think, to have a small dog to call, and say, 'Come! Let's go home now!' and have paws tramp willingly alongside me along the roads and pathways. Even to guard my door at night with a threatening bark to frighten intruders. But I know Missy would not approve, and I would not upset my little companion for all the world.

Below me, on the golf course, I can see Irene and Ralph finishing their game. I can tell it is them, even from this distance, by the fluorescent green of Ralph's shirt, and the pink brim of Irene's sun visor. Ralph puts a possessive arm around Irene's shoulder as she plans her next shot.

When I first moved into the village, newly widowed, I was invited to play golf. At that point in my life, I was trying new things, accepting all invitations, determined not to sit alone and mope. One of the single men, a widower, took me under his wing, taught me the basics. Although I liked being out on the course on a fine day, enjoying the sunshine and exercise, somehow I couldn't work up much enthusiasm for hitting a little ball around. I didn't take it seriously enough for my teacher. I didn't remember to clean his dead wife's golf clubs. I was apt to daydream and plan paintings in my mind, instead of keeping score. He became impatient with my giggles and lack of skill, and when it became apparent that I was not interested in partnering him in any other kind of more intimate games either, he gave up on me, and adopted the next fresh widow arrived in the village. There is always a steady supply.

After I handed back his wife's clubs, I decided to focus on my painting, bought Missy from a local breeder and settled into my own, sedate rhythm. The rhythm that has been jostled into disjointed chaos by Mr Ralph Furnace.

I take out the phone from my pocket and dial Bob's number. 'I'm so worried,' I complain. 'Irene's looking ill. I think Ralph is poisoning her.'

It is a lie. Irene looks as fit as a fiddle pacing after her golf ball. At this stage I will do almost anything to obtain a resolution to this unending turmoil in my life.

*

It is amazing to me how comforting good, hot, simple soup can be. How it warms the oesophagus, calms the spirit, nurtures the soul. As I sip this hot chicken broth, a restrained piano sonata plays on the radio. Andante con mobile. A little acceleration up the treble clef. A progression of chords: a world of ordered sound, with peace at the centre. The major chord, a thing of harmonic beauty, pleasing to the ear. What could be better on a cold evening than to be snug inside while the wind blows leaves around the gutters, howls through the she-oaks on the empty golf-course, and sneaks around corners, looking for crevices to invade?

The music progresses to the second movement, modulates to the minor key, takes on the worried attitude of the grail-seeker, the adventurer, the redeemer of the lost. It proceeds, agitato, to the development, the fortissimo cadenza, the resolution of the bad dream and soothing rediscovery of the initial thematic motif. The modulation back to the original key; the homecoming to the tonic note. *Fine.*

I notice that my pulse has quickened, my breathing is more

laboured. I have become more alert during the excitement of the music. So much drama for a quiet evening at home! I laugh at myself and take another mouthful of soup, which has cooled to drinkable temperature. I fish out a sliver of chicken meat from the bottom of my bowl and feed it to the ever-attentive Missy.

The phone rings.

'Eileen?' It is Irene.

'Yes,' I reply. 'How are you?'

'Fine. Feeling a little arthritic in this windy weather…but Ralph is massaging my ankles for me…such a dear. I just wondered…I know that you're without your car…do you want to come to the shops with us in the morning?'

'How kind of you to think of it,' I reply. 'Yes, if it's no bother…I would be grateful…'

'See you about nine then,' Irene replies. 'Ralph! Don't!'

I hear them laughing, the slap of a hand on skin. After we say goodbye, I bend over and pick up Missy for a cuddle. She is clingy these days, since the break-in, and always ready to snuggle in any warm lap or bed. I check the house, run my bath, turn on the electric blanket. I have a new novel to read, and will hibernate in my boudoir with Missy, while the wind howls.

*

Note pushed under Irene's door, 9 a.m. this morning: *Dear Irene, Susan came home late last night with my car, so I won't need to come shopping with you and Ralph today. I'm driving Susan to the train station. She's organised her job and accommodation, and she's moving to Canberra straight away. Talk soon, Eileen.*

*

Recorded message on my phone this afternoon after my return home: 'Eileen, it's Ralph. Irene has a chill and she's in bed taking paracetamol

113

and fluids. I must go to Sydney and sort out some business. Would you look in on her tomorrow? Thanks. Be back in couple of days.'

Second recorded message on phone, same day: 'Eileen, it's Irene here. Don't take any notice of Ralph. I'm perfectly OK. I don't need looking after. I'll call you tomorrow.'

Third message on answering machine, same day: 'Eileen, Ralph here. I called Irene but there's no answer. Is everything all right there?'

Still standing at the phone table, the phone rings, and I answer it straight away.

'Eileen, it's Ralph.'

'Again?' I laugh.

'I'm so worried about Irene.'

'I'm sure there's no need…' I reply.

'Listen, there's some tonic we purchased in Cambodia from this wonderful herbalist, amazing chap, in our bathroom cabinet.'

I bristle inwardly at his appropriation of Irene's bathroom cabinet as his own. 'Yes?' I reply.

'Will you make sure she takes thirty millilitres of it morning and evening? Thanks. You are a champ. And ask her to answer the phone, won't you? Thanks.'

I hang up, go straight to my china cabinet and retrieve the spare key. If Irene is sleeping, I will let myself in quietly and check on her. I take with me a small flask of liquid vitamins from my own bathroom cabinet. If I am going to administer anything, I want to know what it is. I somehow feel responsible, having fibbed to Bob about poison, to get him working more diligently on the case. As if Ralph had read my thoughts.

Irene is sitting up watching TV in bed when I arrive, the volume up much too loud.

'Ralph phoned me,' I explain.

'Wretched man,' she laughs. 'Although it is nice to have someone worried about you.'

I go into the bathroom, find the bottle Ralph has described, half-full of pale noisome watery stuff. I tip the contents down the sink. I rinse the bottle well, and neatly fill it halfway with the vitamin liquid I have brought in my pocket.

'He wants you to take your tonic,' I say, bringing the bottle and a medicine cup to her bedside. 'Night and morning.'

'Yes, yes, I am taking it, as recommended. But it doesn't seem to help at all. I do feel rather ill…but probably just worn out with pre-wedding excitement.'

'Irene, I know you're a doctor, but…shouldn't you consult a GP?'

'Yes, yes, if I'm not better soon, I'll go and get some blood tests done…but I'm sure it's just fatigue. Nothing really specific in symptoms…'

I make her some tea and toast, say goodbye, go home to unpack my shopping.

7

Masque

Reluctant to go back to the aquatic centre, I look up and find the locations of sea pools dotted along the coastline. On a breezy spring day, I drive out to the closest ones, and find one to my liking. As the weather warms up, everyday I drive there and swim laps, revelling in the sea swell and the old freedom it represents.

My skin feels tighter on my limbs, more resilient after bathing in the cold seawater. I feel confidence return in my stride as I walk down the stone steps to the moss-rimmed pool. I am not worried, as perhaps I should be, about falling and breaking bones. I know the benefits of my new swimming routine far outweigh the risks.

I stick to the pool, although I allow myself short brisk walks along the beach on the hard wet sand. I do not trust myself in the open sea. Once beyond the breakers, falling into that calming, familiar rhythm, I may never turn back to shore.

I haven't told anyone except Susan about my swimming. I suppose I should – but just now it seems like a tentative, early-stage love affair, when to speak of it might make the whole thing less or more than it is; overstate the importance, or somehow make it seem trivial. If any neighbour has noticed my car going out each day at the same time, no one has mentioned it to me. Usually, this sort of regular outing at our age indicates a series of medical or therapeutic appointments. These might be gossiped about behind my back, but etiquette demands that the speculating friends wait to be told health news, however good or evil the tidings may be.

So for the moment, swimming continues to be my secret activity. The waves beckon with a soft sloshing rhythm as I walk towards the pool. These welcoming waves are a constant friend in my life, more enduring than parents or husband, more constant than children.

Ralph seems surprised that Irene is fit and well on his return from Sydney. I am not, and I kick myself daily for pouring the 'tonic' down the sink instead of sending it in a postbag, as I had sent the suspicious cylinder, to Bob.

He has confirmed, after much nagging from me, that the cylinder does indeed contain an illegal substance, although he cannot say more at this time. He doesn't like to say too much on the phone. 'You really must stay out of this, Eileen,' he warns. 'This man is dangerous.'

Irene is well, that is the main thing. I am on the alert, though, for any opportunity to gently question the wisdom of her marriage…any word or hint I can drop at a percipient moment that might change her mind.

Annette drops around regularly, pockets reeking of sardines, maintaining her relationship with Missy. Annette would dearly love to come to the wedding, but Irene is adamant that there are to be no guests, just the two witnesses.

'Ralph doesn't want a big fuss,' she explains. 'Neither do I.'

'Well, I suppose he has done it twice before,' comments Annette. 'One could get bored of the ceremonial side of things. I suppose. But I love weddings!' she enthuses. 'You will take photographs, won't you? I must see you in your wedding clothes.'

Irene baulks a little, at the mention of Ralph's prior marriages.

I take my chance. 'Oh, is Ralph divorced?' I ask innocently.

'Oh…no, a widower, I told you that,' Irene replies.

'Yes, the first wife died, I know…but the second?'

'Her too… Twice he has lost a wife.'

'Cancer?'

'I can't recall…too painful a subject… Ralph did everything possible for both of them, second opinions, overseas doctors, alternative therapies…'

'One is reminded of Oscar Wilde…' says Annette vaguely.

'Wilde? I don't see how. Ralph is not…'

'Losing one parent is a misfortune, losing two parents, carelessness? Is that how the line from the play goes?' Annette, like a dog with a bone, won't give up on this thought. Bless her, I think.

'There is something in that,' I agree. 'Coincidence or…'

'Stuff and nonsense!' says Irene irritably. 'The poor man suffered dreadfully with grief. Even now…'

'You'll know best,' I agree. 'No one knows Ralph as well as you.'

To ease the tension a little, and perhaps allow Irene to dwell on various thoughts that might be circling like crows in her overwrought mind, I offer glasses of chilled white wine to my visitors. Irene accepts gratefully.

Annette declines. 'I'm an abstainer,' she states. 'My parents never touched a drop their entire lives.'

'To each his own,' Irene says.

'Indeed,' I reply. 'Third time lucky.' I hope that something will happen quickly to prevent this marriage. I cannot keep my silence much longer, when I know that Irene is in danger.

*

At the supermarket, pet food is on sale, so I buy two large bags of cat food to leave with Annette when she cat-sits. Rather than carry them around by hand, I drive straight to her house to leave them there in preparation for Missy's stay while I am at Irene's wedding. Luckily, Annette is at home. I have rarely been invited in: it is usually Annette who does the visiting. As I walk through her tidy pale blue living room carrying the bags, I notice piles of delicate fabric on her dining table.

Coming back, I look more closely. 'Annette, these are exquisite!' I exclaim, holding up a daintily smocked baby dress.

There are half a dozen more on the table, some finished, others nearly so.

Annette smiles. 'Yes, I have a little talent in sewing,' she admits. 'The nuns taught me well.'

'Do you sell them?'

'Yes, proceeds to the orphan fund. Mostly on commission these days. Fashions for children have changed so. But some mothers still like something traditional for the baby's christening day. Word of mouth, you know…and sometimes a flower girl dress…'

'I really am very impressed.'

'It keeps me busy of an evening. There's such rubbish on television these days.'

I am itching to place an order, thinking ahead to a baby that Elise and Mike may one day produce…

'You're thinking of a possible grandchild?' asks Annette.

I had not realised I was so transparent.

'Best not to think too far ahead,' she says gently. 'Many a slip betwixt cup and lip. We don't want to jinx them. Or count our chickens.'

I laugh out loud.

'Do you remember,' Annette says abruptly, 'that moment in your forties when you suddenly realised life is short?'

I nod.

'Well, now I realise that it's actually too long,' Annette continues. 'Too long and too lonely. The evenings,' she whispers. 'Just too many and too long.'

'Do you have a radio?' I ask. 'I find the classical music station very soothing.'

'Oh no,' says Annette, smiling. 'Music is too dreamlike, too apt to stir up untidy emotions… I need a mental challenge or a problem to solve, threads to count or a row of numbers to organise.'

'Yes, painting can do that for me,' I reply. 'Working out the creative problems of a picture.'

Impulsively, I give her a brief hug. She allows this for a moment, then gently disentangles herself.

'I have a nice pattern for a little boy's romper suit,' she says. 'I'll find it. Doesn't hurt to be prepared: first babies are often boys.'

We part easily, in good humour, Annette to work on her smocking, me to feed Missy and grab a bite to eat in front of the evening news.

Then I go to my bookshelves and pull out a photo album. I find the photo I am looking for, of Mike dressed in a smocked romper suit, sitting on a knitted rug spread on the floor. There is a similar picture of Susan in this standard baby pose.

I take both the photographs out of the album and prop them up in my painting area. I prepare good quality watercolour paper on stretching boards and begin painting watercolour remembrances of my babies. I am not usually a portrait painter, but feel able to tackle these sweet chubby cheeks and smiling lips. If there was ever a suitable time for sentiment, this is it. These hours before going to Sydney are usefully filled. Annette is not wrong. Keep busy.

Now that I have broken my self-imposed taboo of swimming in salt water, I find myself in urgent need of it, can't miss a day without feeling the strong tidal pull of desire, the addiction of the cool, green seas lapping on my porous skin, hydrating my soul like a desiccated sea sponge finally moistened by the incoming tide. Of course, this is why I have stayed away so long: that inherited, puritan belief that something which has such a hold on me cannot be good; that desires must be controlled and denied; self-discipline valued above self-indulgence, et cetera, et cetera. Discipline being ingrained in me from childhood. That was one of the reasons for my success as a long-distance swimmer. What my rigid parents didn't realise was that, along with self-discipline and a finely tuned physique, they were producing a habit so powerful it was likely to overwhelm me. I came to need the sea swimming, to care about it too much; and when my parents were killed, I blamed myself, punished myself by denying myself the one thing that gave me pleasure above all else.

Howard knew something of this, or suspected. I would swim a little on holidays, but he kept a close eye. I think he knew the beckoning, calling rhythm was still strong in my limbs, my chest, as I breathed in salt and exhaled ecstasy, and that I wanted above all to stroke and kick and dive out into the ocean, into oblivion and eternal rest with the merfolk, in whose existence I totally believe. In my fevered dreams, I am one of them, after all.

I cast off my clothes and pull on the navy blue swimsuit I bought that first day at the aquatic centre. Annoying in its tight elastic straps and leg holes, I have deliberately aged it by repeated machine washes on a hot cycle. It has become looser, smoother, less resistant. More like an old friend. I lift each pliable strap over my shoulders, where bones protrude in pleasing symmetry. Susan is right, I have lost weight and gained muscle tone. This should be enough reason for a woman in her seventies to pursue exercise. I should stop punishing myself for the pleasure.

I used to try and swim in a measured way, when my children were at school. Drop them at the school gate, then walk to the local swimming pool to swim laps. But in that small town where we lived, people noticed everything: it became common knowledge among the gossips that I spent my time loafing around at the pool instead of devoting myself to housework, cooking, community groups, all the common virtues required of married women in that small-minded town. There were even suggestions that I was meeting men at the pool – nothing could be further from the truth, but as soon as I heard that, I buried my cossies with shame in the bottom of my wardrobe, became a cleanliness fanatic, and spent my days dreaming up inventive and peculiar food combinations from the limited stocks in the local supermarket. Not long after that, I met and became friends with Jennifer, who gave me watercolour lessons, and mentored me to a semi-professional career in botanical illustration. Swimming became a forgotten part of my life.

Today, though, as I drive into the car park beside the beach and the irregularly shaped rock pool, formed by a combination of natural rock formations, carved stone and filled-in concrete sections, I feel more alive than I have for decades, feel that a missing piece of the jigsaw puzzle has fallen back into place. I stand for a moment at the top of the stone steps and breathe in the crisp, fresh breeze. I send thanks upwards, to who ever is in charge up there, and feel myself grow larger in courage and calmness. There may be storms ahead, but I will manage. I walk down to the pool between the lime-green mossed rocks and notice a starfish in one of the little pools filled by the outgoing tide. I wish for a camera, so that I could take a reference photo to paint it later on, but will have to rely on memory.

*

As well as losing weight around my middle, my hands and face have lost their chubbiness. Various people in the village stop me on my walk and ask, 'Are you well?' with concern. Others say 'My, you are looking good, Eileen,' and this is a boost to my self-esteem. A little bolstering never hurt anyone. I am thinking of a new, shorter hairstyle…but haven't taken the plunge yet.

I noticed one day that my rings nearly slid off when towelling myself after a swim: so I now leave them at home when swimming. I also take them off to do the dishes. Trouble is, I keep forgetting to put them on again, and where I have put them. Many widows do stop wearing their wedding rings, I know – but I still FEEL married to Howard. Not to wear his rings feels like a betrayal, and I certainly don't want to lose them by accident. Maybe I had better have them resized? But who knows if this weight loss will be permanent?

As I get ready to go shopping today, I look for my rings, but I can't locate them on my dressing table, or in the bathroom, or on the kitchen counter. Missy is no help. Oh well, they must turn up sooner or later. When they do, I will put them on a chain around my neck.

*

An opera company is doing a regional tour, performing *The Merry Widow* in local venues. Annette is keen to organise a theatre party: she has lobbied to get part of the ticket sales for one of her charities.

'You must come, Eileen,' she says. 'You're such a music lover.'

Actually, I do not like opera, and I find that some musicals grate on my nerves. When my radio station features opera, I turn it off. Instrumental music is my thing: screeching and caterwauling about lost love is not.

'I don't know…it will be a late night…I don't think –'

'Not late! No. And it is such a good cause…and all your friends are going!'

I shake my head. But I give Annette the money for a ticket. I will have a headache or something on the night of the performance.

As it turns out, everyone I know IS going, and Irene offers me a lift. I give in gracefully, and get a little dressed up for the occasion. I put on a pretty calf-length dress in layered chiffon, with a matching jacket. I even put on high heels. Missy looks at me suspiciously as I tap across the kitchen tiles. On a shelf above the stove I have a matching set of vintage Bakelite canisters. I reach up and lift down the one labelled SAGO. I haven't ever cooked sago in my life. There is packet of unopened green tea inside. I lift that out, and a circle of cardboard the width of the canister. Underneath, there is a calico bag. I pull open the drawstring and take out Aunt Mabel's pearls.

The pearls are old: a long rope of evenly matched real pearls. Aunt Mabel lent them to me for my wedding day for 'something old' and 'something borrowed'. She had rethreaded the broken necklace herself, using silk from her sewing box, for the occasion. When she died, they were specifically left to me in her will, although as sole beneficiary they would have been mine anyway. I took this to imply that they were important to her. Although she never actually said, I think they were handed down by her mother. I had them valued once – even with the amateur restringing, the figure the jeweller quoted took my breath away. I put them around my neck, put the canister back on the shelf.

Missy circles my legs and complains as I shut her away in the laundry for the night. 'Sleep tight, Missy,' I croon. 'See you soon.'

Irene and Ralph are prompt. Soon we are in the foyer of the local community centre sipping champagne. Irene compliments me on my outfit.

'Nice pearls, Eileen,' says Ralph, leering at my chest. 'Must be worth a penny or two. Are they real?' Without asking, he lifts the end of the pearl string and takes one of the pearls beneath his teeth.

Instinctively, I slap his cheek. His head yanks to one side: this jerk of movement snaps the fragile old silk. Pearls slip, one by one, slowly and then in an accelerating stream, down my body and bounce on the parquet floor.

Annette screams. 'Don't move, anybody! Don't step on Eileen's beads!'

'Fool, they're real pearls,' snaps Irene. She makes everyone stand still, swigs the last of her champagne and goes around the floor, picking up the pearls and putting them in the glass. When it is full, she fills another.

Other people are helping too. Stunned, Ralph and I are standing still like statues. I lift my gaze from the floor to his smirking face. He slowly rolls out his tongue, where a single pearl sits on the crimson flesh. He swallows.

I am tempted to hit him again. But of course, I don't. Irene comes up with the loose pearls. I put them all in my handbag.

'What is it with you two?' Irene asks. 'Why on earth did you cause such a scene, Eileen?'

'Me? It was Ralph…'

'Ralph was simply admiring your pearls,' snaps Irene. 'And yet you took offence.'

'He has swallowed one.'

'Don't be absurd.'

'Ralph is a thief and a con man, Irene. He's after your money.' As soon as I blurt this out, I regret it: it is nothing but the truth, but this is neither the time nor the place for confrontation.

Irene is silent. The look on her face is steely – she turns and takes Ralph by the arm. Together they walk into the theatre. The gong is sounding for the beginning of the performance. I go to the box office and surrender my ticket, in case anyone wants it, call a taxi and go home alone.

*

I don't see anyone at all except Missy for two days after the pearl debacle. I go out by myself, take my pearls to a jeweller for professional restringing, fully intending to send Irene the bill. I clean out my pantry, my saucepan cupboard and even the low shelves under the sink. I am hoping that in this process of spring cleaning, I will find my lost rings.

The phone rings a few times, but I don't answer. If it is important, the caller will try again. It occurs to me that somehow Ralph might have pickpocketed my rings, if I have left them lying about. Not that they are worth much money – their value is sentimental. He wouldn't get much for them in a pawn shop…but maybe he would just do it to aggravate me? I search even harder, and don't do any painting for days, even though I have a commissioned illustration to finish for a gardening magazine.

On the third day, the doorbell rings. It is Irene.

She hands me a pineapple upside-down cake, still warm from the oven. 'Peace offering!' she trills. 'It's all right – the villain isn't with me.' She smiles widely, perches herself on a stool at my breakfast bar. Suggests I make coffee.

I step over the mess of saucepans and cat food tins on my kitchen floor and fill the kettle.

'Ralph has explained,' she goes on, 'that you and he…have a certain attraction…you are probably feeling confused and jealous…of me and Ralph – no, don't interrupt! Let me finish. I just want to say, let's put it all behind us. We're grown-up people, after all. You must get over this. Ralph is devoted to me and although it might be painful, he has no eyes for any other woman.'

I am speechless. I make coffee and cut two huge slices of cake.

Irene takes my silence for agreement. She chatters on about inconsequential things.

'Irene,' I say, finding my voice at last, 'I really don't have any interest in Ralph at all. You must believe that.'

'Eileen, you can't fool me with that innocent look of yours. I've noticed that you aren't wearing your wedding ring any more. Find your own man. Ralph isn't interested in you.'

All I can do is shake my head. 'I've lost my rings…they're too loose…'

'Oh, don't make up pathetic excuses,' Irene says. 'There's no shame in looking for a companion. But it won't be my Ralph.' Irene kisses me goodbye on both cheeks and assures me there is no ill feeling.

Missy appears in the hallway as I close the door.

'Well, Missy!' I say. 'What do you make of that?'

Of course, my rings eventually turn up, once I have stopped looking. When I eventually sit at my easel to finish my work-in-progress, to sort out the yellow tones on a watercolour of daffodils and green foliage, there they are, the wide gold wedding band and the modest diamond solitaire, chosen with Howard so long ago, when we were young and hopeful and thought the best life could bring us was still to be had – my simple rings, casually looped over my favourite squirrel-hair brush, drying bristle-up in an old marmalade jar. I must have taken them off when doing that messy splatter-technique piece, now dried and propped against the windowsill. Ralph hadn't stolen them. Just my silly imaginings. Perhaps I have painted him in rather too dark overtones. Maybe he isn't such a villain after all? Life in the village has quietened, there has been no recent trouble. But…no! There is evidence against him, too much evidence, and too much ill will in the village for it to be all in my own mind. And Bob did warn me…

To break this line of thought, to prevent it souring my afternoon, I switch on the radio and am charmed by the cheerful lilt of Prokofiev's *Peter and the Wolf.* The music, which I have not heard since my children were small, speeds the work along. I decide the cadmium yellow flower trumpets are looking OK, add some titanium white highlights. The green stems and leaves need softening. The colours are so cheerful, they need careful handling, or the total effect will be too jarring to the eye. A touch of French ultramarine should do the trick.

I work steadily through the afternoon. It is nearly 6 p.m. when I finish, satisfied I have done a competent effort for this commission. I tidy up, make sure Missy is secure in her laundry basket and can't run over my work, pull on a jacket and leave the house for a brisk walk before dinner. I twist the rings on my finger as I step through the dusk, their cool presence on my age-spotted finger at once both familiar and strange. I shall not lose them again.

*

I went swimming early this morning, rings safely stored in the sago cannister, ignoring an unseasonably cold wind and staying too long in the sea. I came home and thawed out in a hot shower; ate tinned soup in front of boring daytime TV. Missy climbed on my lap, and we dozed together through the afternoon. Too bleak outside now, I decide I have had enough exercise and won't go out and walk today. I pick up a drawing pad and listlessly sketch a scene of cliffs and rocks and ocean, hatching in the contours of waves, darkening the peaks with extra lines, highlighting the cliffs with dramatic contrasts. I add the small head and one uplifted arm of a swimmer in the distance.

The phone rings.

'Come for dinner,' says Irene. 'Ralph has made a huge pot of beef bourguignon.'

'Ralph?'

'Yes, he's a mad keen cook, didn't you know? He does all our meals now.'

'I don't think so, Irene. It's so cold out.'

'Nonsense! It's only a few steps across. Put on your woolly hat.'

'I'd really rather not…'

'Now don't be one of those stay-at-home types, Eileen! I won't take no for an answer. See you at six.' She hangs up.

I could disobey and stay in. What would she do? Come over and frogmarch me there? Wouldn't put it past her. I sigh as I contemplate my drawing. Is that how Ralph is going to do it? Poison Irene through his cooking? What would he add to the food that would leave no trace? Dare I eat his food? I run a comb through my dishevelled hair. I look in the wardrobe for a presentable jumper to put on over my stay-at-home skivvy and jeans. I am certainly not going to dress up. To annoy Irene, I do put on a knitted beret over my unstyled hair and wrap myself in a pashmina.

As I knock at Irene's front door, there is a pervasive odour of onions and wine. Irene greets me with a kiss, grimaces at my hat and leads me to the candlelit dining table which is set for four.

Ralph is playing the gourmet behind the kitchen bench in a striped apron and rolled-up shirt sleeves. 'Glass of red?' he offers enthusiastically.

I am given a glass of wine and a bite-sized piece of home-made bruschetta. I am just about to ask about the fourth setting, when Dr Alex Banks comes out of the bathroom, smoothing down his wet hair.

'You know Alex, of course, don't you, Eileen?' Irene asks. 'He joined us for golf today.'

It is true, I have met this affable man at Irene's house before. He is a colleague of Irene's, younger than she, who has frequently dropped by to stay the night and play a round of golf whenever travelling up the coast. I don't know for certain, but I suspect he and Irene are old flames. I suddenly wish I had dressed up a little or stayed home. Irene should have warned me. What does she think she is doing, matchmaking? Throwing me her cast-offs?

'Yes, I'm once more enjoying the benefit of Irene's couch,' Alex remarks. 'How are you, Eileen?'

'Eileen has a spare room,' says Ralph. 'Maybe you'd be more comfortable at her house tonight?'

'It's my studio,' I say hurriedly. 'Full of painting gear and smelly rags.'

'No, no…wouldn't dream of imposing,' laughs Alex. 'The couch is very comfortable. I'll be up and gone early in the morning. And it is only one night.'

I take off my beret and wrap, settle at the table. Alex and I chat sociably over carrot sticks and beetroot dip. Irene helps Ralph serve the meal; there is talk about current affairs, golf, politics. A little medical conversation about cataracts: Alex is an ophthalmologist. I admit it is a welcome change to the usual, insular gossip in the village. The men are polite to each other, if a little formal and stiff in their comments. Irene is full of praise for the quite ordinary food and invites us to compliment Ralph on his cooking. I accept a second glass of wine but make that my limit, or I will suffer with headaches later. I eat a little of the beef dish, tasting it tentatively for unexpected flavours, but mostly move it around on my plate. The bread is a safer option. Dessert is a store-bought gelato, so I eat that without qualms. I don't stay for coffee.

'You'll see Eileen safely home, won't you, Alex?' asks Irene.

'Don't fuss, Irene. It's only a few steps,' I say.

'I would like a little air,' says Alex gallantly. As we walk across the road, he says, 'I was surprised to find Ralph Furnace installed in Irene's house.'

'You know him, then?'

'Know of him. It's a small world, the hospital and medical scene.'

I decide to confide a little. 'I'm afraid he's not someone who should be trusted.'

'Well…he left his last job under a cloud,' says Alex. 'Some question of embezzlement, although I don't know the details.'

'Not nearly good enough for our friend Irene,' I state. 'He's a widower twice over, who preys on lonely women. I've heard such stories! I think she's in real danger.'

'Love is blind,' states Alex. 'I…have no doubt that she is in love.'

'We can only watch and wait and hope her eyes will be opened,' I say sadly.

We shake hands at my door.

He turns to go, but then spins round. 'If you're really worried about Irene, call me,' he says, handing me his business card. 'I can drop in uninvited for a round of golf and see what that chap is up to.'

*

These plastic café chairs are grouped in the three primary colours: red, yellow and blue. The type of colours children's paints come in. Strong, bright, unnatural. I wonder about the choice the interior designer has made, what effect was intended. Happy abandon? Childhood greed? As if eating were the new recreation: the café as adult playground.

Conscious of my new, trimmer figure and not wanting to jeopardise it, I order vegetable soup as I wait for Joan and Annette. We have arranged to meet here at the shopping centre and buy a joint wedding present from the Orchid Society for Irene and Ralph. None of us have a clue what to choose – I have steered Annette away from her idea of hand-knitted his-and-hers golf sweaters. This afternoon will be a chore. I have been swimming this morning, and have arrived earlier than my friends. I take a slurp of the hot soup, nibble a little buttered sourdough. What is a suitable wedding present for people of mature age? Glassware? Irene has plenty. Linen? Ditto. Gift card? Boring. I hope Joan has some ideas. We could be traipsing about all afternoon.

I am halfway through my bowl of soup when Joan and Annette arrive in a commotion of noisy conversation.

'You were out early this morning, Eileen,' remarks Annette. 'I rang your bell, but you were out.'

'Yes, I had some errands to do.' I reply. I have still not told about my swimming. 'You know, odd things I have put off much too long. Have you had any ideas for the wedding present?'

'Needn't worry about the present,' says Annette. 'It's all off.'

'What do you mean, all off?'

I must contain my impatience as the waitress takes Joan and Annette's orders for black coffee and lemon tart, cappuccino and black forest gateau.

'Irene and Ralph have quarrelled,' says Annette triumphantly. 'I heard it all, as I was out walking this morning. Door slamming, screaming, cursing… Ralph got in his car and careered down the road at breakneck speed. I doubt if he'll be back.'

'Poor Irene,' I say.

'Lucky Irene, if you ask me,' replies Annette.

'She'll be so upset,' says Joan. 'Even if Ralph is no good, she does love him. Should we go over? Or call?'

'I'll phone this evening,' I say. 'Let's give her some privacy first.'

'There was nothing private about their argument,' scoffed Annette. 'The whole village heard.'

Joan and I look intently at Annette. Is she going to tell all?

Annette shifts in her red café chair uncomfortably, clears her throat. 'I didn't hear everything that was said,' she says. 'But there was one name, repeated often enough to be unmistakable.'

We wait.

Joan prompts: 'The name?'

'Rachel,' smirks Annette, taking a large forkful of her creamy gateau.

*

I phone Irene's number about six o'clock that night. I let it ring and ring, but there is no answer. There is one light burning, but that does not mean she is at home: all of us are apt to leave a light on, so as not to come home to an empty, dark house. I watch and listen until bedtime, and beyond – but there is no sign of Irene.

Missy wakes me with a brush of her whiskers on my cheek. It is an overcast morning: I have overslept. There are sounds outside now, car doors, footsteps, voices. I peek out the window, observe Irene and Ralph loading luggage into their cars. I dress hurriedly, brush my hair and try and look presentable enough to go outside. If Irene is going away, she is likely to tell me first: this is her normal habit.

Sure enough, about fifteen minutes later, the doorbell rings. Irene is on my doorstep, dark glasses on, car keys in hand. She doesn't waste time with formalities. 'We're going to Sydney,' she explains. 'Some business to attend to.'

'Business?'

'Yes, lawyers to see, accountants to consult, wills to write. Pre-wedding stuff.'

'Wills? Irene…'

'Yes, wills. I bet you don't even have one. Everyone should look to the future, even if the thought is painful.'

'Of course I have a will,' I snap. 'And my children have power of attorney.'

'My next of kin is a second cousin thrice-removed,' says Irene. 'But marrying will change that.'

'Are you sure about this marriage, Irene?'

'Nothing could be more certain. It is what I have wished for.'

'You're driving?' I ask.

'We need both cars,' she explains. 'I'll be returning before Ralph.'

I reach out and touch her hand. 'Irene…is everything all right?'

'All right? Yes, perfectly all right,' Irene affirms, but does not remove her dark glasses.

'Annette thought…'

'Annette is a busybody who should mind her own business!' Irene declares, an impatient foot scraping a line on my tiled floor. 'Whatever she told you is exaggeration. All couples have spats. We're no different.'

'As long as he hasn't –'

'I love Ralph and we're going to be together for the rest of our lives,' Irene says. 'The sooner all you old biddies get that settled in your minds, the smoother life will be.'

All I can do is nod, promise to look after the house, wish her a safe trip.

'Come on, old biddy,' I say to Missy, after Irene is gone. I fill the kettle for tea, put tuna in Missy's bowl, and think about poaching an egg. 'Just us old biddies here,' I say, putting bread into the toaster.

I am fairly certain that Irene's dark glasses concealed a black eye.

*

'I've had an idea,' says Annette.

I swallow the last of my cappuccino, look around the golf club bistro. It is almost empty this midweek morning. The first players have not yet come in from their session. Annette and I have met Joan here, before her tee-off. Neither of us play, but Joan is quite good, albeit a little reluctant to start playing again without Larry. I have been telling them about Irene's black eye.

'An idea about what?' I ask.

'How to help Irene, of course,' says Annette, taking a bite of her date scone.

'OK, what's your idea?'

'Well…Ralph is a ladies' man, right?'

'I guess you could say that.'

'You should make a play for him.' Annette's eyes are dancing.

I cough into my napkin, take a sip of water.

Joan is laughing out loud.

'How would that help Irene?' I ask. 'It would only make her mad at me.'

'It would expose him as an opportunist, a faithless cad.'

'I don't think so. Anyway, why pick on me? You could smooch up to him.'

'Oh no, I haven't any experience in flirtations… You're the youngest and slimmest – sorry, Joan, it's true. Anyway, Joan is still mourning Larry…' Annette trails off, her plan sounding more and more bizarre.

'Ralph came on to me,' states Joan.

Annette and I stare at her.

'It's true,' Joan says. 'The day after my family left. He came over with flowers – just him, not Irene – and hugged me. But it was more than a hug.'

'I don't believe it!'

'What did you do?'

'Trod on his foot. Hard. I was wearing golf shoes, with spikes.'

'Good for you! See what a bastard he is!'

'You should tell Irene,' advises Annette.

'She wouldn't believe me,' says Joan.

'We believe you,' I say.

The waitress comes over, sensing gossip, and hovers. I give her something to do by ordering three more coffees. When she is out of earshot, we discuss all sorts of pros and cons of trying to tell Irene about Ralph's behaviour, but we can't think of any good way forward.

'I still think you should lead him on just a little,' Annette says to me. 'Let him kiss you. Joan can hide and take a photograph to show Irene.'

'I would rather kiss a rattlesnake.'

*

Annette phones. 'Haven't you heard anything from your son's future father-in-law?' she demands. 'Aren't the police going to act? I was sure they'd arrest Mr Furnace before the wedding and save Irene from a fate worse than death.'

'Bob says the evidence is still being collected,' I reply. 'We must wait.'

'What do they need? We could go snooping…' suggests Annette.

'We must not get entangled. Bob was definite about that. We have to trust the professionals.' I reply.

I feel just as frustrated about the situation. Helpless to save my friend. My earlier relief in sharing the problem with Bob has evaporated. As the wedding day gets closer, my despair and helplessness is escalating. The police don't seem to be doing anything at all about Ralph. At times I think I have imagined all these things, that Annette and I have made mountains out of molehills.

I find Dr Alex Banks's business card in my wallet. He is someone to trust, surely? Someone with no good opinion of Ralph, and a long-time friend of Irene. Plucking up courage, I dial his number. Just an answering machine. Well, he is a busy man. I don't leave a message. Missy paces the room, as if smelling a thunderstorm in the air.

I am praying for a miracle.

8

Counterpoint

Annette and Joan breeze in on Sunday morning, fresh from church. Irene and Ralph have gone off early to play golf, with much noisy discussion and laughter. Missy and I have been observing the Sabbath in our own quiet way, in my courtyard.

'Praise the Lord, my sins are forgiven!' chants Annette. 'Yours too, Eileen,' she adds with a wink.

'I don't think Eileen has any sins,' says Joan, sitting herself on the garden wall in the sun.

Annette and I look at each other, remembering her mother's engagement ring, which is now securely locked away in a safety despot box at the bank.

'I said a special prayer for Irene,' she whispers to me while Joan inspects my orchids.

Missy stretches, arches her back and settles again in my lap.

'If you want tea, you'll have to help yourselves,' I say. 'Missy has decreed it's a day of rest.'

'Oh no, we had a cuppa after the service,' says Annette. 'Full as a goog. There was chocolate cake too.'

'We just thought you'd be interested in the afternoon concert the church is organising next month,' says Joan. 'We thought we'd go – it's all here in the newsletter.' She places a photocopied pamphlet on my table.

They know me well, these two. Music is the thing that will draw me in, the balm of my soul and of blessing to my heart. It is true, I sometimes go and sit in the little community church, enjoy the calm and the music. I can tune out any discordant notes of do-good-isms that occur if I am an infrequent member of the congregation. Live and let live.

We gossip for a little while about village affairs, then they go, reminding me of our arrangements for Wednesday. Annette's son is coming, and Joan and I are her moral and practical support.

'It will be fine,' I reassure her as she trots out the side gate. 'Just you wait and see.'

*

'We're going skiing.' Irene has phoned to ask me to watch her house.

'Skiing?'

'Yes. There have been some good late falls at Perisher and Ralph wants to strut his stuff on the slopes.'

'Irene…is this wise?' I ask. More bravely, I continue '…at your age?'

'Don't be a worry wart, Eileen. I won't do anything stupid.'

I can tell from her tone that she is going along with this trip, but has no real interest in it. Is this how Ralph will kill Irene? Push her down a mountain? I know that they have written new wills. I must think fast – give Irene an excuse to cling to.

'Irene, you know that painting in your living room of Sydney Harbour…I've always admired it…'

'Yes. What about it?'

'Well…you said…you once said you'd leave it to me in your will.'

'So I did. What a funny time to bring that up. You really want it?'

'Were you serious about leaving it to me?' I ask.

'Yes, a promise is a promise… I wish you'd reminded me last week.'

I can hear Ralph in the background.

'Just a minute, Eileen…'

I can hear them talking.

'Ralph, I don't think I can come with you…last-minute wedding stuff… Eileen reminded me… I'll call you later, Eileen.' Irene hangs up.

I do watch the house while they are away. But Ralph goes skiing alone. Irene goes to Sydney to see her solicitor. For the time being, all is well.

*

Joan and I are in Annette's gleaming kitchen, making salads and plating cold chicken and quiches for the visitors' lunch. Annette has been tidying her living room, hovering by the freshly cleaned window, fidgeting with the curtain tie-backs, fussing about dust.

'Annette, they're not coming to rate your housekeeping skills,' I say.

'I just don't want them to think I'm a doddery old lady who can't look after herself.'

'They won't. How about a coffee?'

'Yes…I might – No! Here they are! There's a car in the drive!'

Joan and I clutch each other's shoulders, holding our breath.

'He's here…oh! He looks like my father…so tall and the same way of walking…and that woman – must be his wife, carrying flowers… such lovely red roses – she has a nice face…that young woman, their daughter? And oh, there are two little girls! Twins? No, one is taller…' Annette goes to the front door.

We watch from inside as Annette and her son embrace. Her great-granddaughters skip around them in a circle. It is going to be all right.

*

I've just finished a Skype session with Susan, and am sipping a mug of instant coffee, fooling about on my computer with a game I really don't understand. They are meant to improve your mental capacity, these brain games. I think this one is just scrambling MY little grey cells even further. I picture a plate of discoloured scrambled eggs… There's a little PING from the computer, and a request to Skype. It isn't Mike or

Susan. They have both warned me about cyber-scams and imposters, and I am about to delete it when I take a second look at the name: A. Banks. I wonder. I decide to risk it and click ACCEPT.

As the image pops up on the screen, I recognise the harmonious features of Dr Alex smiling at me. Thankfully, I have been out this morning to the hairdresser, and look fairly presentable. (It doesn't do to let your daughter think you are letting yourself go and not coping. I scheduled my talk with Susan for after my salon trip on purpose.)

'Hope you don't mind the intrusion,' he says. 'I looked you up, saw you online, and thought it would be friendlier than a phone call.'

'I'm delighted to see you,' I reply. Then worry that this reply is too effusive.

'I just have a short break between patients,' he says.

I notice that he seems to be in his office; there are framed university degrees on the wall behind him.

'I'll get straight to the point. I've been looking to invest some savings, and I discussed it with Irene…'

I get a dull sickness in the pit of my stomach. I think I know where this is leading. I nod. 'Not with Ralph…?'

'…not with Ralph. But Irene must have talked to him about it, and next thing I know Ralph is on my doorstep with the prospectus of an investment scheme. I took the paperwork, just to get rid of him. He has been hounding me ever since.'

'You surely wouldn't trust…'

'No way would I let that man near my money. I'm sorry I trusted Irene, but she IS an old colleague. My accountant looked the scheme over, and warned me off it too. Ccan you give me the name of your detective chap so that I can add this fuel to the fire?'

'Delighted.' I get out my address book (the paper version) and read out Bob's name and phone number.

We say goodbye, and I thank him, and we make those sort of polite promises that acquaintances make to be in contact again soon. As I power off the computer, Missy looks at me with her piercing blue eyes.

'Why should he?' I ask the cat. 'Why should Alex notice my new hair-do?'

Missy turns and stalks into the kitchen. As I fill her bowl, I reflect, Susan didn't comment on my hair, either.

*

'I'm thinking of taking a trip,' says Joan. 'Have you ever been on a cruise?'

'No,' I reply. 'I don't think I'm the cruise ship type. Too many people in a confined space.'

We are circling around the edges of the golf course, strolling together, getting a little gentle exercise. It is late afternoon: the golfers are completing their games, heading into the clubhouse. A flock of white cockatoos sweep in to graze on the slopes, as twilight descends.

'I'm not sure that I am either,' replies Joan. 'You hear such tales. But I don't think I want to travel alone. Nice to have someone to share experiences.'

'A group tour? What do you want to see?'

'Maybe South America? Japan? I don't know exactly. I just want to go places that are quite different…new cultures, new smells, new vistas…'

'A complete change.' I stoop to pick up a fallen gumnut that takes my fancy. I already have a few wild flowers in my hand, am creating a composition to draw later at home.

'Well, yes. You know, Larry and I travelled quite a lot in Australia, but he never wanted to go further than that. I have the money, and I think now is my chance.'

'Before it's too late, you mean.'

'Exactly. I miss Larry…every minute of the day…but that doesn't mean I shouldn't do what I want, for a change,' Joan asserts.

I nod. 'I still miss my husband, too. But Howard, bless him, was the one who wanted to travel, not me. I'm happy pottering around at home with Missy and a box of paints.'

'You don't ever feel hemmed in?'

'Not really. As long as I have my music, and something to draw. Although I could be tempted by some of those classical music tours in Europe…you know, birthplace of the composer, concerts in the grand castles, that sort of thing.'

'Yes…and a cruise down the Rhine. We could do that together, if you like.'

'But I'd have to leave Missy.'

'Annette might…?' Joan suggests. 'They seem to get on.'

'But would Annette feel slighted if we don't ask her to come too?'

'Only one way to find out. I'll do some gentle probing,' Joan replies. 'I think you and I would be compatible travel buddies, don't you?'

I agree. Joan is the most pleasant and easy-going of women. Friendly but not intrusive; active but not frenetic. 'As long as you don't mind if I linger too long at a ruin, working in my sketchbook,' I say.

'I can be very annoying, Larry used to say, trying to find the perfect angle for a photo,' laughs Joan. 'I think we'll understand each other perfectly.'

We have completed our circuit and are back where we began. I head home to Missy, Joan in the opposite direction to her empty villa. I am wondering if I shall sketch in charcoal or use some new pastel pencils I have yet to open.

*

'I haven't been loafing,' says Annette, unwrapping a long hand-knitted scarf from around her neck and piling it into her capacious tote bag. She pulls a sheaf of papers from the bag and thrusts it at me. 'I made a list! An inventory of all Ralph Furnace's evil doings.'

I look at the purple carbon pages in dismay. Annette's idiosyncratic documents are legendary within our Orchid Society. To her, all information technology is evil. Satan himself dwells within each microchip, steals souls from personal data and chants the code that makes the computers whirr and beep. Don't even get her started on the symbolic meaning of certain logos in the shape of fruit.

Annette will not have a computer in her house. She is wedded to her manual typewriter, circa 1946. She has inexhaustible stores of carbon paper (goodness knows where she even buys it these days) and types the society minutes in triplicate, the most legible parts being the emphatic full stops and underlining that are characteristic of her literary style. Many times, minutes have been passed, unread, simply due to the unfortunate quality of the copies, and a common desire not to upset the secretary. The most modern device Annette will employ is the photocopy machine at the local library. We keep hoping that she will run out of carbon paper and use the photocopier more often – but her carbon copies just keep coming.

'I've kept the originals,' Annette says, 'in a safe place. 'There's a copy there for you, and one for your police detective. Don't leave them lying around…we don't want Irene to see!'

Annette has come early to the Orchid Society meeting, which I am hosting. I have set out china mugs and teaspoons, sugar bowl and serviettes, savoury snacks and home-made cake. Together we arrange extra chairs around the living room. Annette places a smudgy blue copy or a pale photocopy of the minutes on each chair, and members begin to arrive.

It isn't until early evening, after the last people have left and I have put the house back in order, that I turn on my favourite music, make myself a mug of soup and sit down to read Annette's list. It isn't that hard to decipher – a numbered list of actions, observations, dates and snippets of reported conversations with village residents that build up a character portrait of Ralph since his arrival in our midst. Annette must keep a diary, I realise – or have an excellent memory – to have this level of detail at her fingertips. My first impulse had been to fob her off with some excuse, but this list may be quite useful to the police. But I can't show them these amateur typed pages. At first glance, they will also think the document is the folly of an elderly and eccentric mind.

Pouring myself a fortifying glass of red wine, I go to my computer and begin transferring Annette's list into a document that I can email to Bob.

I am mindful that the problems of working with my son's future father-in-law on a criminal matter in which I have a personal interest is fraught with dangers. I do not want Elise and her family to think Mike's mother is a loony old woman. Suspicions are easily formed, easily expressed, but very difficult to substantiate. I have wondered if I shouldn't deal with some other member of the police force, am concerned that Bob is simply being polite and not really doing anything to investigate Ralph at all.

I refill my wine glass. Just about finished. I save the document and think about taking a shower to rest my aching shoulders. I start the spell check –

The doorbell rings.

I tuck the carbon lists under the pile of journals on my desk, minimise the document. Missy is at the window – I check through the chink in the curtains to see who is at my door. Irene and Ralph.

'Recovered from the meeting?' enquires Irene as she air-kisses me, despite the fact it is merely a few hours since we saw each other.

Ralph plants a wet kiss on my cheek, and I can't help instinctively wiping it off with my sleeve. I have never liked the smell of beer.

'We had dinner at the golf club,' says Irene. 'Thought you might have done the same.'

'No, just had a little soup,' I reply. 'Happy to be alone after that fracas.'

There had been a disagreement between Irene and Annette about the management of the annual competition and the amount of prize money to be offered. Irene thought an increase was necessary, but Annette firmly held that people entered for the status of winning, not for the prize money.

'Annette is living in the dark ages,' Irene declared.

'Let's not revisit it,' I implore. 'Missy has only just recovered from the ordeal.'

They sit down uninvited and seem ready to socialise. I offer coffee and cake left from the afternoon tea. In the kitchen, Irene and I find clean mugs and plates, laugh about the suggestion that someone had made about designing orchid hats for members to wear at our annual show.

'At any rate, we shan't be here…most likely our cruise will be that month,' says Irene.

'A cruise?'

'Yes. We thought it would be nice to do something for ourselves without any obligations.'

I express surprise: Irene has always scorned retired people and their pleasure cruises, travelling only with a purpose and never in the tourist haunts.

'Yes, just a holiday. Ralph, show Eileen the cruise we're taking…'

I drop the coffee mug. It shatters on the tiles and splashes black coffee on Irene's white trouser leg.

Ralph is sitting at my computer. He has the web page of the cruise operator on the screen. His face turns to me, as blank as a newly-primed canvas. His impenetrable eyes look up and down my body, as if I were a carcass in a butcher's shop.

We both know he has seen the list.

*

'Computers!' Annette is in a state of righteous anger. 'Tools of the devil!'

I have taken the coward's way, confiding in her by phone. She answered on the first ring, despite the late hour. I hold the receiver a little further away from my ear, to mute her exclamations. I just know she is quoting scripture at me.

'I don't think it's safe for you to be alone,' she says a little more quietly. 'I'll come over.'

'NO!' I am a little more forceful than I intended to be. 'I'm fine. And he didn't find the originals. I'll sleep with them under my pillow.'

'Call your detective man,' she begs. 'At least do that.'

After Irene and Ralph left, in a hurry to cleanse Irene's stained trousers, I had locked my door and raced to the computer. My file had been deleted.

*

It is after midnight. But I no longer care about social niceties. Despite my brave voice to Annette, the look I saw on Ralph's face really has me rattled. I call Jan and Bob.

Jan answers. Bob is out. She is up late, painting – she wants to hear everything. In her kind, earth-motherly way, she talks my fears down from near hysteria to watchful caution. 'We'll drive up tomorrow. Meet us for breakfast at that beach café? Good. See you then. Call me back if you need a friend! I'll be working all night…'

I can't thank her enough. Missy snuggles on my bed, and I pretend to read, but actually I lie alert and worried almost until dawn. I dress and leave the house before the sun has reached my window. I take Missy in her cat crate, seat belt fastened around it to keep her secure. If anyone asks, I will say it is a routine vet visit. I am not going to let Mr Furnace harm Missy again.

*

I'm early at the beach café. It is cold, but if I didn't have Missy with me, I would calm myself by swimming in the lap pool. As soon as the café opens, I buy a takeaway latte and sip it sitting in the car with Missy, spinning it out until Jan arrives. The sun is warm, through the car window, and I find myself dozing.

A rap on the window rouses me. It is Jan. I leave the window down a little. Missy is sleeping, and I can see the car from the café balcony where we find a table with a view.

'Bob is so sorry, he couldn't get away,' Jan apologises. 'Give me the list, and I'll make sure he takes notice.'

We read through the list together while we wait for our breakfasts to be cooked. Jan makes notes, clarifying any of Annette's points that were smudged or badly worded.

'This really is worth the effort,' Jan says. 'You friend has an eye for detail. She must really care about you and Irene to go to so much trouble.'

She is right: Annette may be eccentric and fixed in her views, but she has a loyal and courageous heart. What have I done to really help Irene? Nothing, except fret and worry through sleepless nights.

'Come down to Sydney and stay with me,' urges Jan. 'You have Missy in the car. We can go straight there.'

I shake my head. I can't leave Irene – she is in danger and I would never forgive myself if I were away and something happened. I can watch. I can call the police at any sign of trouble. An ambulance if… I shake my head and look at the horizon, glimmering with morning light.

We linger over eggs benedict and more coffee. We watch surfers paddle out to find a wave. We work our way to happier topics of conversation: Jan has brought photos of her elder daughter's wedding to show me. We discuss Elise and Mike's plans. By the time we say goodbye, I feel that my panic was all a bit foolish. I go home via the supermarket and buy sensible things. I stop by the local library (Missy is content in her crate with a small snack of sardines) and borrow a good, long, historical romance that will absorb me long enough to bring sleep when night falls.

*

The phone rings early next morning. Missy and I have slept well, risen at our normal hour and begun cleaning the house.

It is Bob. 'Your friend's list,' he says. 'Very thorough. What's the lady's name? I'll send someone to interview her…'

'Annette Simpson. Number 24…around the bend…other end of the road…' I read out her phone number. Annette will be thrilled and frightened in equal measure to be interviewed by a detective. 'Should I…'

'No, no need for you… Thanks, Eileen. I'll be in touch.' Bob is not one for long conversations.

I go back to my chores, fill a bucket with hot suds and mop the sticky coffee stain on the tiled floor with gusto. I wish I was washing Ralph Furnace out of our lives.

My house is a neat as a pin, and Missy is enjoying a snooze near the front door in a patch of sun. Still in cleaning mode, I find a chamois and bucket and go outside to clean my car.

Halfway through the job, a sudden rending of metal and screeching of tyres followed by an almighty thud causes me to drop my bucket and run down the road. On that bend that she always takes too fast, Irene's car is crumpled head-on against a telegraph pole. As I run, I take my phone from my pocket and dial emergency. Another neighbour reaches the car first and is helping Irene from the wreck. There is no one else in the car. Blood is oozing from her forehead. Someone brings a chair from their front patio and we lead Irene to it, sit her down, listen to her words.

'Brakes didn't work... I'm all right...just banged my head...'

Another neighbour brings a blanket, wraps it around her shoulders.

I hold her hand, which is shaking. 'Irene, where is Ralph?' I ask.

'Golf. Ralph's playing golf...'

As the ambulance arrives, Ralph runs up the road, still hauling his golf clubs. He makes a fuss, kisses Irene over and over, is the one to climb into the ambulance and go with her to hospital. There is nothing I can do except go home, finish my car cleaning, phone and leave a message for Bob about the accident.

*

'Don't be absurd. How is Ralph to blame?' Irene retorts.

I have placed my hastily purchased arrangement of pink carnations on her bedside table, taken a perch on the uncomfortable hospital visitor chair.

'The brakes failed, it is as simple as that. My fault if anyone's, my car...I should have checked...'

'Who used the car last?' I ask. 'Ralph. Who took it for the last service? Ralph. Who has driven you everywhere else lately in his own Mercedes… Who suggested that you take YOUR car yesterday…'

'Eileen, you're talking about my fiancé. The man I love. Who loves me.'

'Does he?'

Irene holds her head in her hands. 'Please leave. Take your flowers and go. I don't want to be lectured and I won't listen to any more of it.'

I stand and walk to the door, leaving the carnations behind. 'Irene,' I say softly, 'Ralph may love you, but he has murdered two women. Be careful. Maybe he can't help killing what he loves most.'

*

Irene is released from hospital after three days. Her head wound is healing and the risk of concussion over. She and Ralph keep to the house, but a steady stream of visitors can be seen entering and departing, carrying gifts of flowers and casseroles.

I don't visit. I take Annette's lead and compile a comprehensive list of every fact I have discovered about Ralph and send email bulletins to Bob daily. I have stopped worrying about being a nuisance. Irene's life is at stake.

*

It is Ralph who comes to my door. I speak with him through the security screen.

'Eileen, I want to make a truce. I…love Irene. I know that you think I'm a cad…unworthy of her. It is true, there are some things in my past that I'm ashamed of. But that's all behind me. I would never hurt Irene. She brings out the best in me. I was so frightened when I saw that ambulance, the crushed car… I was afraid I'd lost the best thing that ever happened to me. Please say that you'll make up with her. She's grieving about your quarrel. I promise that I really do have her best interests at heart. Come for coffee at our house tomorrow morning? Please?'

I went. What do they say? Keep your friends close, and your enemies closer.

*

Despite all my misgivings, on the night before Irene's wedding, I am lying in the snug spare room at Jan and Bob's house on the northern beaches. I can hear the soft sound of the distant waves pounding the shore, the sounds of possums roaming their bushland garden. Not flash, but extremely comfortable, their home is just to my taste and I feel glad that Mike has chosen his future bride from this lovely family. My clothes for tomorrow are ready: I am to be collected by taxi early in the morning, to meet Irene at her hotel and thence to the harbour-side wedding location. Uneasy but strangely calm, I have discussed my fears about Ralph with Bob and Jan over and over.

I have been plain spoken to Irene about Ralph. I have put my fears aside for her sake. She has asked me to be witness at her wedding, as planned, despite my concerns. I do not want to be there. I could simply refuse – but would that be the action of a friend?

After my tiring day, sleep is claiming me, and I'm not unhappy when I hear the gentle patter of raindrops on the steel roof. 'Maybe the wedding will be cancelled,' I console myself sleepily. I listen to the radio news on the hour. 'Sydneysiders should prepare for more hazy mornings in the coming weeks,' says the announcer. 'High humidity levels combined with cooler nights will create ideal conditions for fog to develop.'

Next thing I know, it is morning. I miss my cat's wake-up nuzzle on my hand. I hope Missy is faring well at Annette's house; a little part of me hopes that she isn't enjoying her holiday too much. I don't want to lose her affections completely to Annette and her sardines.

Reluctantly I get ready and dress in my finery for the wedding, still wondering what I could do to stop Irene from making this tremendous mistake. In these modern times, I don't suppose marriage celebrants still ask that traditional question: 'If anyone present should know just cause why these two people should not be joined…'. If they should, would I be able to trust myself not to call out?

*

'Here's the bridesmaid at last,' says the best man, adjusting his comb-over, checking the effect in a wall of mirrored tiles.

The fog has slowed down traffic across the city. My taxi has taken an age to reach the hotel. Irene, Ralph and Peter, the best man, are standing anxiously in the lobby.

'Not a bridesmaid, not even matron of honour,' I object. 'Friend and witness.' I kiss Irene's cheek and admire her outfit.

'Witness this,' says Ralph, taking Irene in his arms and kissing her long and deeply.

'Isn't it bad luck?' I ask. 'For you two to even see each other before the ceremony?'

'A load of old tosh and superstition!' Irene declares, straightening her neckline. 'This isn't that sort of wedding.'

'And yet you're wearing white,' I remark.

'I've always been told it suits me…don't you think?'

I agree Irene looks dazzling in her very expensive outfit. I know. I helped her choose it.

'You look lovely too, Raelene,' Peter says to me.

'Eileen,' I say. 'Eileen is my name.'

'They say that in the Middle Ages, bridesmaids were decoys,' Ralph says. 'In case of abduction. So that kidnappers would be confused, and not manage to steal the bride.'

'I'm not a —' I begin.

'In that case, they should be wearing identical dresses,' Peter comments.

'You have it wrong, Ralph,' I interrupt, suddenly remembering an obscure fact from my schooldays. 'It was ancient Rome, and the maids were present to confuse and outwit the evil spirits.'

'Mmmm…vestal virgins,' says Peter.

'I hardly think —' says Irene.

'In any case, bridesmaids are meant to protect and help the bride,' I state. 'Which I will gladly do. Even though I am just a witness…'

'I seem to remember that in romantic Victorian novels, the bridesmaid went with the couple on their honeymoon,' Irene says. 'A month-long grand tour of Europe. In case the bride needed help and support.'

'Now there's a thought!' laughs Peter. 'A threesome, eh, Ralphie?'

This comment doesn't please Irene at all. Ralph knows enough not to run on with the joke.

'As much as I adore our dear friend Mrs Rickaby,' says the lying toad, 'I need my bride all to myself, Pete. Romance on the high seas just for two.'

The plan is for a simple harbour-side ceremony, lunch on Peter's yacht, then he and I will disembark, leaving Irene and Ralph to their honeymoon on the borrowed craft.

'Mrs Rickaby…?' murmurs Peter. 'You're a widow? You and me could paint the town red after this shindig is over, eh, Raelene?'

'I'd really love to…Paul,' I say. 'But I have a family commitment.'

Peter checks his reflection in the wall mirror again and adjusts his cravat. 'Well, well, let's get this show on the road,' he says, with a wink. 'Ladies, your chariot awaits.'

*

I can't help but be pleased that the weather hasn't played its part – a promising long-range forecast of clear skies over the harbour has been overtaken by a white, bridal fog that curls around lampposts, tucks its arms around buildings, weaves its way over and under wharves, and shrouds boats in blankets of misty haze.

They go ahead with the ceremony as planned. Irene's silk pantsuit with orchid bouquet, tone-on-tone of white on a little half-moon of sand where the marriage celebrant recites poetry and asks the two to promise fidelity.

Ralph is solid and substantial in a nautical navy blue blazer beside

Irene's white. I stand to one side, Peter on the other, forming a tiny semi-circle of humanity.

We don't linger on that small beach in the fog. We board the yacht moored at the private jetty, toast the couple with champagne, and head out into the harbour, hoping to escape the fog. Irene and Ralph are unusually solemn, I am watchful; Peter is absorbed in his duties as captain of the craft.

Perhaps to lift our mood, Ralph turns on some music. 'Something you'll like, Eileen,' he says, turning up the volume of the familiar strains of Mozart.

I shiver.

'Cold?' he asks.

I nod. In my light summer dress, the damp air is eating into the pores of my skin, cramping my muscles, chilling my bones.

Ralph takes off his navy blazer and puts it round me. The tailored wool is heavy on my shoulders, swamps my body with its bulk.

'Put it on,' encourages Irene.

I slide my arms into the sleeves. Ralph slides the brass buttons into their neat buttonholes.

Irene turns and points to a tiny patch of blue sky appearing over the bridge. Her back is to us, as she looks to the east. She chats to Peter about the weather conditions.

'I know what you really are, Ralph,' I say quietly. 'And I know what you've done. If you hurt a single hair on Irene's head, I will –'

'You'll what, Eileen?' he sneers. 'Set your cat on me?'

In the next moment, Ralph deftly picks me up and places me, as if simply removing a book from a shelf, into the briny harbour. As I sink into the cold, strangely welcoming waters, his breathy, whispered words, uttered so close to my ear, echo through my mind: 'Sleep well, Mrs Rickaby.'

It was a shock, I don't deny it, to be one minute breathing air on the deck of the yacht, and the next immersed in cold seawater, dense and opaque, green and populated with creatures of the underworld. Yes, even in Sydney Harbour, life teems below the glinting, impenetrable disguise of reflected light.

As I floated down, weighted by wet wool and surprise, a groper looked me in the eye then scuttled off to a mess of floating weed to find something edible. I was not his dinner – and I hoped it was entirely the wrong time of day to be shark bait. The swift departure of the fish brought me to my senses. I began to kick and swim, but I just kept going down, and I knew that my breath was nearly expired.

The jacket was heavy, unreasonably so. I reached into the pockets and felt fishing weights in the lining, sewed in where I could not tear them out. I fumbled for the buttons neatly fastened down my chest, but they were not easy to undo, catching on the buttonhole stitching. I took a risk at this point, a necessary risk to save my life – I was so angry at Ralph, this emotion fuelled my actions, and helped me, I am sure, to struggle for a solution. The jacket, far too big for me, allowed me to wiggle my arms out of the sleeves into the body of the garment. I then wedged my arms against the lining, and reversed my way out the bottom of the woollen tunnel, like a semi-trailer reversing out of a narrow lane when unable to go further forward.

All this seemed to have taken hours, but it couldn't have, because I was still conscious. I kicked away, in what I hoped was the opposite direction to the yacht, and upwards. I surfaced in deep fog, took a sustaining breath, and swam steadily towards a red spot of light which I took to be a signal or marker of some kind.

There was no one around when I walked ashore a pebbly cove. I climbed the uneven sandstone steps to the well-manicured lawn of a private garden, sat for a few moments to rest on a wrought-iron bench overlooking the view, then went to the house in search of a telephone.

9

Danse Macabre

It wasn't Susan or Mike I rang. I called Bob. He was quick to answer and arrived at the house in a police car with an ambulance following.

'We've got him now,' Bob said, rubbing his hands together. 'And he's too cocky, he's starting to make mistakes. Let's see what his next move is.'

I was taken to the hospital and admitted, but not through the normal emergency process. Under Bob's authority, with a false ID, and feeling rather daring, I assumed the name of Mrs Smith.

I changed into a hospital gown behind flimsy cotton curtains while Bob conversed with the police doctor. Nursing staff came in and out, carrying warm blankets. I accepted a hot cup of tea which helped a lot. Bob and the doctor went out into the corridor. I could hear their indistinct voices but couldn't decipher the words. When they came back, I was examined and pronounced fit and well, if a little exhausted. Bob made detailed notes, took my statement, and told me of his strategy. I was to lie low while police observed Ralph to see what his next move would be. No one would know I was not lying at the bottom on the harbour.

'How did you manage,' asks Bob, 'to float so far so quickly? Did you catch hold of a buoy, or something?'

'I didn't float,' I retort. 'I swam.'

'Quite a distance,' he replies, one eyebrow raised.

'Not at all. Have your detectives look up English Channel swimmers. My name was Eileen Foster then.'

Both eyebrows raised, Bob makes a little bow with his head. 'I had no idea …'

'All long forgotten,' I say.

'Well…rest now, stay quiet, and Jan will come by with some clothes,' he advises.

I have no choice but to obey.

There is a constable outside this bland, single room, guarding the door.

As I lie here on this scratchy hospital sheet, I begin to shake. Delayed shock, I suppose. I wish for Missy's comforting presence. I think about phoning Susan, but just in time, remember that I should check with Bob about the safety of making phone calls. Looking around, I realise that there isn't a phone. And my own mobile will probably be at the bottom of the harbour, or still on the yacht. Instead, I turn the radio dial around and around until I find some Mozart to help me relax, and slide further into bed for warmth, dozing off in the middle of afternoon.

Much to my embarrassment, I am woken by Jan knocking on the door at about six o'clock. She is carrying containers of steaming Chinese takeaway, and my overnight bag. 'You poor thing, what a shock!' she exclaims, giving me one of her generous, earth-mother hugs.

I don't mind. I am in the mood for a bit of cosseting. To think Ralph actually wished me dead! The truth is only just sinking into my consciousness.

She wraps an extra cotton blanket around my shoulders, and we begin on the spring rolls and pork dumplings.

'Bob thought it best I come alone,' she said. 'Girls' night in. Don't want to give your hideaway away, so to speak! We are officially shocked and bereft, puzzled by your absence. We will report you missing, if it hasn't been done by that so-and-so Irene already…'

'I can't believe she's in on it,' I say. 'Irene's my friend.'

'This type of man can hoodwink anyone,' Jan replies. 'Irene may be swept along by passion, or blackmail…or maybe you just didn't know her as well you thought.'

I sigh. 'Thank goodness for friends like you and Bob,' I reply. 'I can't thank you enough.'

'We're family!' says Jan. 'Or near enough. We still have so much to decide about the wedding. When you feel better. Tonight, we can just relax…watch TV…are you fond of Judi Dench?'

Jan and I watch a movie on the small hospital TV high up on the wall, and eat the takeaway food together, exchanging little anecdotes about Mike and Elise, fantasising about their future together.

'I love being a grandma,' says Jan, whose elder daughter already has a baby boy.

'I thought there was no chance of ever being one,' I reply. 'My two have been so slow to settle down.'

'Life throws us these little surprises,' Jan philosophises. 'Sometimes sad, sometimes happy. We must remember to make the most of the happy ones.'

'I agree.'

'More wine?' Jan asks, as she drains the last of her cab sav from a paper cup.

'No, thank you.' I snuggle deeper into the blanket wrapped around my shoulders and think of Missy.

When the movie finishes, we channel surf and come across the late-night news.

'Here's your five minutes of fame!' laughs Jan. 'Although Bob says you've experienced it all before… Why didn't you tell us you were a famous swimmer?'

'A harbour-side wedding in Sydney this morning was marred by a tragic accident,' reports the newsreader. 'A woman fell from the yacht, in which the wedding party was celebrating, and is missing, believed drowned. The missing woman is seventy-one-year-old Eileen Rickaby, mother of two. Search efforts were marred by unusually dense fog in the area.'

Irene is shown in her wedding outfit, talking to police, clinging to Ralph's arm, shaking her head. Ralph looks straight into the camera, and tells the reporter how he jumped off the yacht himself and swam around looking for their missing friend.

'Liar!' I cannot believe my ears.

Irene looks genuinely distressed. I decide to give her the benefit of the doubt. She cannot have known what Ralph was up to.

'Annette will be beside herself with worry,' I moan. 'And all our friends in the village…this will be gossiped about for weeks.'

'It isn't your fault,' said Jan. 'and with any luck Ralph will finally get what he deserves.'

*

In my hospital gown, I stand barefoot on the grey lino and look out the double-glazed window at the city skyline. My head throbs and my limbs are empty of vigour. It is a day with pale grey skies and a haze of brown smoke in the treetops. A mean, menacing sort of sky. The sort of day when you can believe the world is coming to an end.

Somehow, Bob and the police department have managed to obtain a body that has been falsely identified by Susan as mine. (I don't understand how this has been done, and I don't want to know who the poor dead woman is.) Bob has agreed to reassure Mike, secretly, but drew the line at telling Annette I was still alive.

'For this to work, we need it to be realistic,' he had said. 'Grieving friends making a fuss is just what we want. Your Susan is good at acting,' he added. 'Perfectly believable. Has she ever worked undercover?'

'Don't be silly. She's an art historian,' I had replied.

But now, alone, my mind drifts off into strange imaginings. Perhaps her work in Madrid wasn't simply art restoration, as she claimed. International espionage? My Susan? She was always so competent and self-contained.

A funeral service has been swiftly arranged. It will be in Sydney, which is a little unexpected, but perhaps this is better in the long run, as fewer of the village residents will be put through the ordeal. Some, of course, may travel down for the service – is this a test of true friendship? And who will give the eulogy? I try not to think about it, but in the end, Susan promises to video the event so that I can see what happens.

'I'll say it's for Mike,' she says, 'since he can't attend. It'll be a simple service,' reports Susan, in the one phone call I am allowed with her. 'I'll make a short speech, representing me and Mike…'

'Thank goodness we haven't many relatives.'

'…then other people will be allowed to speak if they want. We'll play some of your favourite music…'

'The Mozart lullaby,' I interject. 'That's what Ralph played when he threw me into the harbour. Make him squirm.'

'He's beyond any sort of remorse, if you ask me,' Susan states. 'But if that's what you wish…'

'My dying wish,' I reply.

'Then the coffin will slide away, laden with flowers…'

'White flowers. Roses, gardenias, old fashioned freesias…'

'My goodness, you are a demanding corpse!' says Susan. 'But your wish is my command. The police are paying, anyway.'

'I wonder if Irene will speak.'

'She must, mustn't she? It's all her fault. She must be feeling very guilty.'

'I don't know. Is she in collusion with Ralph? Have I misjudged her all this time?'

'What do you know about her, really? How many years has it been?'

'Well, you do tend to take your neighbours on face value and give them the benefit of the doubt, don't you? Living close together and needing each other for companionship.'

'Have you been lonely, Mum? Has it been too hard since Dad died?'

'Susan, you know I've managed perfectly well. A little loneliness is normal.'

'I've neglected you…' Susan apologises.

'Fiddlesticks. You've been leading your life, just as you should. And I've been leading mine. I don't sit around and mope, you know. I have my painting, and Missy, and my friends…'

'Friends who throw you in the harbour…oh MUM! It could really be you in the coffin. We really could have lost you!'

'Save your tears for tomorrow to make it look authentic,' I say sternly. 'It'll take a bit more than a dunking in salt water to finish off your old mother. I was a channel swimmer, you know.'

'I DIDN'T know!' replies Susan. 'Why didn't I know? Why didn't you ever…'

'Long story that'll keep for another day,' I reply firmly. 'Now, don't forget, I want to know who comes and what happens.'

'OK, I'll do my best. Love you, Mum.'

'Love you too. Talk soon.'

*

The video streaming from Susan's iPhone onto the iPad via Skype is quite clear. The sound is muffled, voices come and go but, on the whole, it is easy to follow what is happening. If anyone asks, Susan will say she is Skyping Mike, who is overseas, and unable to attend. My coffin, as I requested, is laden with white flowers.

'Nice flowers,' I murmur, forgetting Susan can hear me.

'Hush, Mum, you're supposed to be dead,' she hisses. 'Be quiet!'

The strains of Mozart are familiar and dignified. Mourners walk into the small chapel and take their seats, clad in dark suits and sober dresses. The chaplain is dressed in ecclesiastical robes, adding gravitas to the event. Susan pans around the room, and I see Annette weeping into her handkerchief, and feel a sharp pang of anxiety for her. I wish she could have been let into our secret. A well-groomed man comes in alone and sits at the back. Dr Alex Banks. Joan and a group of other people from the Orchid Society sit together on one side. I recognise the aquarobics lady too, but I still can't think of her name. June, no, Jane…no, Janine? No, I really can't remember.

Then Irene and Ralph walk down the centre aisle and sit just behind Susan, who is in the front row with Bob and Jan. Irene is wearing dark glasses. She is in grey silk, a pantsuit, elegant but the right thing for a funeral? I am over-critical, but it IS my funeral, and it IS her husband to blame for it all. She nods at Susan, bows her head. Ralph is looking straight ahead, expressionless. Susan turns back to the front.

The chaplain begins to speak. 'We are gathered here today to give thanks for the life of Eileen Margaret Rickaby,' he says. His voice is clear and somnolent; I approve of his respectful attitude. 'Before we hear from Eileen's daughter, Susan, we have a request from the ladies of the local choral society to present a musical item. Ladies, if you will…'

Susan looks directly into the phone camera with a quizzical look and shrugs.

Annette is one of the women who now come forward. She speaks. 'I had the privilege of knowing Eileen Rickaby,' she says in a tearful but resonant voice. 'For just a few years, we were friends and neighbours. I know that this song meant a great deal to her, and that is why we will sing it for Eileen today.' She steps back into the semicircle of ladies, and nods to the organist at the side of the chapel.

Expecting the sweet measured tones of *Weigenleid*, I can't believe it as they begin the familiar tune of 'Climb Every Mountain'. The camera shakes and I just know that Susan is suppressing the giggles. At least, I hope that she is suppressing them. She knows that this is NOT my favourite song – it is Annette's; funny how people place their own likes and values onto other people when the victims have no recourse. My indignation turns to amusement at the earnest faces and warbling voices of the choristers. I can see the funny side. I am NOT a victim, and laugh inwardly, albeit a little hysterically. What next?

The singers resume their seats and the chaplain restores a solemn tone with a Bible reading, a prayer and a general statement about the facts of my birth, family and unfortunate death. No mention of my swimming career, I notice. Oh well, some secrets go with us to the grave. A few words about the unpredictability of life; about being mindful and living in the moment; about appreciating loved ones while we have them near us. He invites Susan to speak. Susan does me proud; real tears appear in my eyes as she talks about our family. She can keep that speech for the real thing, I decide. Then others are invited to speak: this is the risky part of modern funerals; any madman may disrupt the event with personal grievances and evil nonsense.

Irene shakes her head, will not approach the microphone. I can't believe my eyes as Ralph walks up and takes the microphone out of the stand, holds the cord in the other hand, and paces the little dais, as if he were Tom Jones. Surely, he isn't going to sing, too?

'Irene and I want to express our deep sympathy to Eileen's family,' he says. 'Eileen was a wonderful neighbour to Irene and, more recently, also to myself.'

The congregation is silent, except for an agitated rustling from where Annette and the choir ladies are sitting.

'We had many happy times together,' Ralph continues, 'Irene, Eileen and little Missy her cat, together in the sunny courtyard enjoying morning coffee. That is why I would like to offer this small song in memory of our friend.'

He is going to sing!

I can't believe my ears as the accompanist starts and Ralph begins a rendition of 'What's New Pussycat?'

He is only on the second whoa-whoa-whoa, when Annette leaps to her feet. I can see this because Susan spins around at the disturbance and captures Annette's wrath on video beautifully.

'Murderer!' proclaims Annette. 'Thief! Philanderer! Poisoner of innocent pussycats!'

The organist breaks off with a blur of electronic notes, the chaplain steps forward and takes the microphone from Ralph.

In the stress of the moment, I forget myself. I cry out, 'Oh Annette, I'm not dead!'

Susan's thumb turns off the volume immediately, but it's too late. The people in the first few rows turn and look at each other. Irene slides her dark glasses down her nose and turns to Susan.

Swiftly, a pair of funeral directors, in their crow-like dark suits, take Annette gently but firmly by the arms and escort her out of the chapel.

The chaplain spreads his arms wide, as if to encircle the gathered people with peace, and says calmly, 'Let us pray.'

Bob whispers something to Jan and exits the chapel quietly down the main aisle.

Susan zooms in on Ralph's tanned face, which shows no embarrassment, just a lopsided smirk and a glint of knowledge in his dark eyes. He leaves the dais and follows Bob out of the chapel.

If I am not dead yet, I soon will be.

*

The sight of the hospital lunch makes me feel slightly nauseous – but I shouldn't complain. I turn away from the plate of food and climb out of bed. It is modern and clean, this hospital, but, for a healthy person, deadly boring. I am not to communicate with anyone beyond please and thank you. A young female police constable is stationed outside the door, just in case. ('In case of what?' I asked Bob. 'Never mind,' he said. 'Better safe than sorry.')

Once the video streaming of the funeral had finished, I began playing solitaire on the iPad. All those little faces and the symbols and the numbers lining up, the little click as the cards fall into line…mesmerising. I can see how people become addicted, how the persuasive hope of lady luck being on our side might sway people into bad habits. I have never gambled, always been a saver and a careful planner. Maybe I have missed something? No, just give me a sure thing like a paintbrush and a pencil, and everything will be just fine.

I taste the coffee that has come with the meal, and nibble the digestive biscuit provided on the saucer. Stale. I take another mouthful of the bitter coffee. I hope that Missy is not fretting. I hope that Annette is not too upset.

I shake myself and tell myself to get a grip. Better take a nap; you are still overwrought, I advise myself. I pull up the cotton, open-weave blanket and snuggle onto the squeaky plasticised pillow as best I can. I doze.

A breeze is coming from the open sliding door to the balcony. A little too fresh.

I stir and think about getting up to close the door. But, too lazy to move, I snuggle down further under the blanket. In my mind I hum a few bars of my favourite sonata.

Next thing I know, I am gasping for air. A tight band is wound around my throat, choking me awake and then into semi-consciousness as the room begins to go dark…

A crash through the swinging door as the constable arrives, gun at the ready. She kicks Ralph Furnace in the groin and places her heavy-duty boot none too gently on his chest as he lies writhing on the floor, her pistol to his forehead.

She grins at me. 'Sorry, I was a few minutes late. Spending a penny. Are you all right, Mrs Rickaby?'

*

'I told Bob he was a complete and utter beast to set you up like that,' Jan says. 'I don't care if he is my husband. Stinker. As if you hadn't been through enough already!' She has brought a large bunch of scarlet roses, and home-made chicken soup in a Thermos.

My throat is so bruised, I can barely speak, let alone swallow. Susan sits beside my hospital bed, offering me sips of water, relaying reassuring messages to Mike on her phone. I nod, shake my head, or gesture according to the questions she asks. I am tired but not exhausted; the strength of my visitors is bearing me along.

'But how did Ralph find me?' I whisper hoarsely.

'He followed Bob out of the funeral. Bob led him here on purpose.'

I shake my sore head and shiver uncontrollably.

'I know, it was a terrible risk, and I haven't forgiven him,' says Jan. 'Apparently Ralph used Irene's access card to enter the doctor's car park. He went to the operating theatres and got dressed in scrubs and a face mask…no one challenged him. He slipped in while the constable was in the toilet…coming out she got a glimpse of his back…fortunately she reacted in time.'

Susan hugs me ferociously. 'I still can't believe Ralph was actually trading in biological weapons,' she says. 'Like something out of a TV crime series.'

'Bob says there was enough poison in that cylinder you found to make all Sydney seriously ill,' says Jan. 'If it had been put in the water supply.'

'Why would anyone want to do such a thing?' Susan shakes her head.

'Plenty of terrorist associations with money to pay the right price,' says Jan. 'It seems Ralph would do anything for money.'

'But why kill me?' I moan.

'You weren't swallowing his lies,' Jan says. 'He wanted you out of the way. And Bob says the police needed to catch him at it…real proof of attempted murder. Otherwise it would have just been your word against Ralph's, with no witnesses, that he tried to drown you.'

Irene was there, I tell myself. Irene must have known.

There is a tentative knock at the door of my private hospital room. Annette's head peers around, then she trots in carrying a basket. 'Didn't expect to see you under police guard!' she whispers.

'Don't worry, it's only witness protection,' says Jan, who goes on to introduce herself and fill Annette in, since I can't manage so much talking.

Annette places the basket on the foot on my bed, unties the fastening, and lifts the lid.

'Missy!' I croak, as my little cat is lifted out.

She sniffs the bed, circles around, and snuggles under the crook of my arm. For the first time in days, I begin to think that things will finally come right. Missy purrs.

*

Later on, I am shown the video footage. There are closed-circuit cameras in the hospital car park, the corridors, the operating theatre scrub room, the wards. I see Ralph calmly drive in, use Irene's swipe card to enter the hospital. He walks with quiet authority to the theatres. Changes and scrubs up, places a surgical mask on his smiling face. No one challenges him. He even jokes with some wardsmen pushing trolleys into the lift.

I shiver as I see him walk the corridor towards my room.

I jump out of my chair as I see a skinny woman in a hospital gown sitting on a bed and realise with a start that it is me. What else had I been filmed doing?

Bob fast-forwards the video. 'I'm sorry all this was necessary, Eileen,' he apologises. 'But we did need hard evidence.'

Too hard, I reflect, fingering the bruises on my neck.

'The trial will be another ordeal for you,' Bob says. 'But I know you'll cope. You're the resilient sort. An endurance swimmer,' he chuckles. 'Still can't get over that.'

I shake my head. 'Not so resilient,' I say. 'But I do want to see that man locked away for a long, long time, so that he can never bother Irene or any other woman again.'

*

It takes a while to get my equilibrium back. There are a few weeks at home with Susan, before she returns to Canberra. There will be a trial; Ralph is in custody, bail denied; I try not to think too much about it.

While Susan is with me, I drag out my tub of swimming memorabilia. Sitting together on the sofa, we turn the pages of my scrapbooks, examining the newspaper clippings, the certificates, the photographs, the ribbons. I open the box of medals, and hand her one at a time, describing the swims. Susan has lots of questions, and I do my best to answer.

'Why did you give it up, Mum?'

I take a deep breath and try to answer honestly. To put my grief for my parents into perspective; to understand how long-distance swimming had been as much for them as for me; how their support had been an essential part of the sport. I couldn't quite give voice to the deep knowledge that I somehow knew only on a physical level: that without my mother standing at the finish of the race, on the shoreline, in all weathers in her coat and scarf, with a lantern to guide my wobbly footsteps over the coastal rocks, I wouldn't ever return to shore but swim out in search of Dimitri.

A new peace descends on my relationship with my daughter. When she leaves, it is with a new interest in family history, a pride in my achievements, and a promise to research my past in the national archives.

I don't do much in the way of painting. Just a little sketch of the starfish I saw at the rock pool, with a light wash of aquamarine. I think about branching out into other marine subjects: sea anemones, pipi shells, rock pool finds. Some days, now I have begun swimming again, I emerge from my sea pool, stand and contemplate the changing colours of the sea, plotting which pigments I will use, what types of wash and brushstrokes will be required to render my new vista. I am gathering visions and storing up creative energy, and soon they will converge onto paper.

What are the anchors that tether us to the shore of normal life? When our significant other has been and gone, or never shown up at all? Children, if we have them, and they stick around. Routine; good, absorbing work; companions, pets, music. Sleep and dreams. The rolling waves of the sea. Faith, hope, and starfish.

*

Mike flies in and stays with me for a week before the wedding. He fills up the spare room with his bags and technological paraphernalia; buys me a present of a new computer and spends a lot of time installing it; seems to be calming pre-wedding nerves by eating enormous amounts of food. Missy is upset by the upheaval in the household. She is off her kibble.

He stands at the open door of my pantry, surveying the contents.

'Hungry?' I ask.

He pulls out a bag of salt and vinegar chips and begins munching. It is like having a teenager in the house again: perhaps he has regressed.

'Shall we go out to lunch?' I suggest. 'Or we can get something and bring it home. I need to go to the supermarket.'

'Yeah, lunch…my shout… Any Italian places nearby? I feel like a big bowl of pasta…parmesan…garlic bread…'

'Nervous about the wedding?'

'Just a bit.' He grinned. 'I love Elise. I really do. I'm just worried about the responsibility…of being a grown-up, I guess.' He takes another gulp of chips. The bag is nearly gone. 'Do you think I'll be a good father? Like Dad was?'

'Of course you will. When the time comes.'

'Elise really wants a family. I hope I'm up to it.'

'The two of you will be fine. And little old Grandma Rickaby will stand by to help.'

'I am glad you're OK, Mum,' Mike says with energy. 'That crook! I hope he rots in hell.'

'It's all in the past now,' I say.

'Wish Dad could be here, wish he could know Elise.'

'Me too.'

Mike grabs me by the waist and waltzes me around the kitchen, as he used to do many, many years ago as a boy. Missy watches anxiously from the hallway, then retreats to the lounge. Before we leave, I gently pick her up and carry her into the laundry and settle her in her wicker basket. I will buy her some sardines: perhaps that will reassure her.

*

Cicadas are competing with the string quartet on the radio as I sit at my dining table facing the window with a half-finished cup of coffee, and a small charcoal sketch pegged on my easel, ready for colour. It is for my usual, personalised Christmas card for close friends. The fan is whirring to create a breeze on this still, hot day.

White curtains move silently with each breath of a small breeze.

The cat, reclining in front of the window, high on the back of the wing-backed chair, is extended to her limit, to receive the full effect of fluid air on her body. The curtain cloth is meshed with stars and moons, woven galaxies that lift and shift in the fabric of time.

The afternoon is gentle: without machine noise or traffic buzz, voices or thunder. The folds of curtain move like lungs, filling and refilling with room with languorous thought. Joy may take you unawares: peace comes gently on cat paws and sits behind you on the office chair. You don't notice, until the warmth of feline respiration relaxes the small of your back.

I have been thinking of Mike and Susan as I do the usual holiday things. Make a Christmas cake that I will offer guests, if I have any; buy small gifts that will post easily; place a few decorative festive items around the house. Nothing too big or involved, just a small Norfolk Island pine tree with gold baubles; a simple wreath on the door.

The cicadas, in record numbers, scream their summer message — life is short, get on with it. I ponder the colour palette for my card, experiment on a scrap of parchment. I have in mind the deep blue of night skies, as a background, to be lit by stars of flannel flowers: a local take on the nativity theme, the light that shines in the darkness.

The blue tones have merged: cobalt wash bleeds into aquamarine; is darkened by Payne's grey and shadowed by my charcoal hatching. These are the shadows that we make to hide our secrets. Where we allow evil to lurk. The darkness of night, also the blessed well of rest, the sombre reservoir of dreams, where we can float effortlessly, dive deeper into subconscious seas, swim with unnameable desires. I have masked the star shapes of the flowers to keep the whiteness of the paper. Once the background has thoroughly dried, helped along by my little hairdryer, kept ready for this purpose, I carefully remove the masking fluid. I highlight the petals with cadmium yellow and titanium white. I finish with a touch of gold: it is the festive season, after all.

Missy looks pleased with my efforts. I will take the finished card into town tomorrow to be scanned and printed. I could do this online, I know, but I like chatting with the print shop man about papers and sizes and passing the time of day with a friendly face. He is always glad to have my business, and there is little enough goodwill among people these days.

I find my address book and calculate the number of cards I will need. Thumbing through the pages, I read names of people recently deceased. I will need fewer cards this year. On impulse, I add Dr Alex Banks to the list. Cross out Irene? Or not. Some other friends have stopped posting cards completely, substituting email messages or phone calls. Others go overboard with lengthy typed letters, listing every event of their grandchildren's lives. I will send my simple personalised card as usual, and hope people are glad to receive it. And I will file away the original painting into a scrapbook where I have stored all the others, every year for decades. I hope that Susan or Mike will like to have the book, one day when I am gone.

To protect my work, I put Missy in her basket in the laundry while I go for a stroll in the early evening dusk. It is a calm summer's night; a few neighbours exchange greetings as we enjoy the cooling air. Back at home, I realise that I have left a window open all day – a window adjacent to the deck, so that any intruder could easily enter. After so many months of fear and locking my house against threats, I have relaxed my guard. Winding it shut, I reflect on my calmness of mind, the readiness to experience whatever comes. If there is worrying, I have already done it. If there is grieving, I shall work through it. If there is life, I shall share it. Panic has no place here.

*

I don't usually cry at weddings. I didn't cry at Irene and Ralph's; I didn't cry at Mike and Elise's: I saved it for later as they left on their honeymoon. A week in Hawaii before starting a new job in San Francisco. I am used to Mike being away, living in foreign countries: but it doesn't make saying goodbye each time any easier.

On the day of the wedding, we had breakfast together, Susan, Mike and me, just our little Rickaby family, and in all of our minds Howard was there too, so that we were tinged with sadness as we looked forward to the day. Mike was uncharacteristically nervous, and Susan teased him gently, reminding him to shave and shower, helping him tie his necktie, brushing off his tuxedo.

Susan looked elegant in a little black dress; I was presentable in a peacock-coloured silk ensemble, a scarf draped around my throat, which still bears the marks of attempted strangulation. Elise was fresh and extremely pretty in her simple white gown, carrying an orange-blossom bouquet. The ceremony was held in Bob and Jan's lush garden, in a bower surrounded by iceberg roses. I might have dabbed at my eyes a little when the vows were exchanged.

Bob and Elise were excellent hosts. The reception at their house was friendly and well catered. As I look at the photographs now, it all seems too much, too soon: such a lovely, untarnished day, the wedding and Christmas both come and gone! Another year beginning with all the usual nonsense about horoscopes, back to school basics and goal-setting. It is so predictable, I can't bear to watch TV or read any form of mass media.

Thank goodness for Missy, and for painting. I have a little burst of enthusiasm for sea urchins and other marine subjects. I am trying out a new colour palette and techniques that will offer a little movement and texture to my subject matter. I realise that I have stagnated with flowers and garden painting far too long.

Susan and I plan to visit Mike and Elise. Annette will mind Missy. But we will wait until a few months have passed, until winter comes with its chill mornings and endless hours to fill. In the meantime, I will finally get back to serious painting.

*

In the post today there are three bills, a real estate brochure offering to sell my house, and a postcard from Mike and Elise. It is a standard beach scene with palm trees and hibiscus flowers. They are having a wonderful time and send their love. It is nice to be remembered.

I went to an island once. It was just after Howard died, after I sold our family house and was waiting for the purchase of this villa to go through. Everything was packed up or given away; in storage or disposed of. I was at a loose end – suddenly free of worry and responsibilities. Someone (a neighbour, well-meaning, not a particularly close friend) suggested a tropical holiday. 'Somewhere warm,' she had said, 'away from it all. Where you can let your hair down and relax.'

This was obviously her dream: it wasn't mine. She didn't really know me at all – didn't see that I was not the cocktails by the pool sort of person. But, always easily led, I allowed her to choose a holiday package on a tropical island, a brief getaway, that she said would 'give me back to myself' after 'all I had been through'.

Some women are glad when their husbands depart this earth: I understand that. To be legally free without guilt could be a blessing in disguise for some widows. But me, well, Howard had been my guiding light. I know it sounds corny, but for all my adult life he had been my lover, my friend, my counsel. He kept me on course. I was adrift without him.

I went to the island. I admired the swaying palm trees, walked the white sands. I dressed in new, bright summer dresses (picked out by my neighbour on our shopping trips, while her husband was at home in the garage pretending to fix the mower) and got blisters on my feet from new espadrilles. I lay on the sun lounge by the pool with an unreadable trashy novel that I used merely to shade my eyes from the sun. I sipped cocktails; I attended themed banquets; I went on organised sightseeing cruises. The island was full of couples on honeymoon or wedding anniversary celebrations. I was miserable.

I put the postcard on the fridge and hold it in place with a magnet advertising plumbing services. I say a little prayer for my family. I hope that the New Year brings us only happiness.

*

Irene swirls the ice cubes in her water glass so that they tinkle, and takes another sip. She will not make eye contact with me. 'I'm not sure why you wanted this lunch,' she says. 'The lawyers weren't in favour of it.'

'Lawyers?' I fumble. 'But surely…'

'You didn't think we'd let the charges go uncontested, did you? Of course I consulted the lawyers before being seen in public with you. It could jeopardise everything.'

'Irene, Ralph tried to kill me,' I say quietly. 'Twice. How can you even talk to him?'

'I shouldn't be talking to YOU,' Irene snaps. 'I don't really know why I agreed to come. You haven't been the friend I thought you were, Eileen. Making false accusations, concocting stories against my husband, getting him into all sorts of undeserved strife...'

'Ralph deserves everything he got,' I reply. 'And much more. If he had his way, I'd be lying dead on the bottom of the harbour. And who knows what untold damage those viruses would have caused in the wrong hands? I don't know how either of you can sleep at night. I thought you were a moral person, Irene.'

'Fiddlesticks!' cries Irene, crumpling up her paper napkin and pushing her unfinished salad away from her. 'I promised to stand by Ralph, and I will. If you were any kind of friend, you'd drop the charges.'

'I can't, even if I wanted to,' I reply calmly. 'It's all out of my hands now.'

Irene stands, gathers up her dark sunglasses and handbag, walks away without another word.

I am left alone at the table with the seagulls hovering, hoping for scraps. I throw them a couple of my unwanted chips. The harsh reflections of light on glass, on stainless steel, on ceramic plates, the rims of a plate rack, the glossy surface of onion rings dressed with oil suddenly feel overwhelming. To my left, the beachfront is starting to get busy with families spreading towels out beneath beach umbrellas, children hopping on one leg, then the other, anxious to swim in the surf, grandmothers holding the hands of toddlers, walking to the tide line with buckets and spades, ready to build castles from the wet sand. A bald newborn in her mother's arms...I remember that weight of warmth and love. I try to imagine what emotional pay-off Irene gains from her relationship with Ralph. I guess everyone likes to be needed.

It could be as simple as that. I order coffee, and drink it surveying the scene. I am past anger: the emotion pulsing through my mind is more an amazed bewilderment at Irene's behaviour than rage.

An hour passes, and I sip a second coffee as I mull over past events, still trying to make sense of the whole sorry affair. The afternoon sky is that deep, dense azure that allows no clouds and forgives no sins. The blue that doesn't forget. I consider how I would paint it with acrylics on a wide canvas, as wide as the earth. A sky that is a slow burning memory of the world and all our troubles. Finally, the squawk of a still-hungry seagull rouses me from my thoughts and, although the café-restaurant is not busy, I realise I should go and let the staff clear my table. As I pay the bill for both lunches, it occurs to me that the personal cost of the rift with Irene will be long and ongoing: that whatever calm dignity I can muster will barely be enough to tide me over. Investments in friendship are the most vulnerable and irredeemable of assets. I tell the waitress to keep the change.

10

Weigenlied

It's a mess. I finally admit to myself that this half-finished, watercolour orchid sits awkwardly on the page, is out of scale and the colours have bled into areas that were meant to remain white. It must be trashed. Too hasty; too distracted; too bothered about other things to settle calmly and work, I have wasted a good sheet of watercolour parchment and feel totally cross.

I peel off the tape holding the misshapen flower picture, with all its defects, on the backing board, turn it over and tape it down again, smoothing the surface. It is really good-quality paper; I can't see any of the orchid coming through. With a soft pencil, I sketch free-form shapes, allowing myself some creative space to try and settle my mind. I draw more shapes, marine monsters of unknown nomenclature, shining treasure chests buried in the deep. Carried away by fantasy, I swipe a cobalt blue wash to create waves that I will later enhance with gilt crests. No deadlines, no demands, no rules – under these conditions, my painting flourishes.

I spend the rest of the evening engrossed by this picture, end up totally lulled by the creative release. As I splodge on a reckless amount of cadmium yellow, I make a sudden decision to ask Joan, a keen photographer, to take over the orchid journal illustrations. Photography will be much quicker, and I really have almost done orchids to death. 'And they me,' I tell myself. I can't look at an orchid without thoughts of Irene and Ralph erupting in my head. Joan is coping well with her loss, and perhaps a little distracting activity will appeal. I will ask her tomorrow: definitely time for a change.

There is something about being the survivor of a crash. The one spared. The one left to carry on. The one who knows they should also have been taken. The guilt of being still alive; the responsibility of living appropriately when others have had their lives cut short. Notice how I have these thoughts in third person: how I distance myself from the idea that my life has been on borrowed time.

How could I keep swimming when there were no parents waiting on the shore with a dry towel, a helping arm to support my aching limbs, a ready drink for my dry throat? How could I even keep on living with no father to guide my career, decide my next challenge, organise a sponsor? It was all too hard. After the fatal crash, I went to live with my only surviving relative, a great aunt. It was in her house that I recuperated from glandular fever, roused myself enough to attend secretarial college, found work in an office. Howard worked there, too. As if exhausted by the responsibility of me, Auntie Mabel died three months after my marriage. Her race was run.

When Howard died, just weeks into his retirement, it was abandonment all over again. All the lovely plans we had made, come to nothing. Nothing but memories, memories of his warm skin and his strong hands, always ready to steady me.

These days, as I step from the rock pool, dripping and shivering in the offshore breeze, there is no one to hand me a towel, rub my chilled spine, chap my cold fingers in their warm hands. Perhaps I have finally found the courage to swim alone, to prepare for the final lap, and head home.

*

Irene comes to say goodbye. She steps away from my intended embrace; dodges my cheek kiss. I have been watching the removalist truck since this morning, being filled with her household contents by brawny young men in khaki shorts and singlets.

'I'm all packed up,' Irene says. 'Except the orchids. I won't have room for them in the unit: you and the other Orchid Society members had better take what you like, sell the rest on a street stall.'

'Oh!' I reply. Unsure whether to thank her or protest, instead I stammer, 'I'm so sorry you are leaving.'

'Well, least said soonest mended,' chants Irene.

Some old saying trotted out for an awkward moment, I have no idea what she intends it to mean.

'I'll need the key,' she says.

'The key?' I say dully.

'My spare house key. The one I gave you. I'll need to hand it in,' explains Irene.

'Oh…of course, silly me.' I go to the china cabinet and fish the key out of my mother's Spode sugar bowl. As I place it in her hand, she turns to go, but I grasp her arm and ask, 'And mine? You have my spare key?'

'Oh. Not sure where that got to.' She looks swiftly away, and then looks me straight in the eye for a moment. 'But you HAVE changed the locks, haven't you?'

As she walks away, I feel that I have been excised from her life, swiftly, neatly, completely. No scalpel could have made a cleaner cut.

Inside my house, behind the closed and locked front door, I hear the truck start up and rev off down the street; Irene's own car start and follow with a softer drone, and a sudden screech of tyres as she takes the bend much too fast. I am thinking of some half-remembered lines about haste, about good fences and neighbours… I have been spending too much time with Annette and her platitudes, I reflect. Not usually a solitary drinker, still today I go to the fridge and take out a bottle of sav blanc I have had chilling, pour myself a full glass and lift it to Missy, saying quietly, 'Absent friends.'

*

It is Annette's birthday; she is having an afternoon tea party. All the remaining Orchid Society members are here: Annette's choir buddies, church friends and many other village residents. Her villa and courtyard are both packed with people, seated on chairs, standing in small groups, gossiping and laughing. Her son Tony and his family have organised the party; his wife has made a superbly iced, two-layer cake. On the top there is a large 80 in silver, framed with delicate apricot-coloured orchids modelled from sugar. The cake is proudly in the centre of the lace-covered table where people are putting gifts. Joan and I place ours with the growing pile. There are flowers, books, other parcels still unwrapped. Joan has enlarged, and framed in silver, a photograph she took of Annette and Tony on the day they were reunited. I have opted for a personal touch, too: framed one of my floral watercolours that Annette has previously admired.

'I didn't realise you were eighty,' I say to Annette as she hands around tiny, triangular sandwiches filled with cucumber and cress.

'Yes, older than I look, eh?' Annette smiles. 'No more secrets.'

Tony hands me a cup of tea, which I take carefully. Annette has got out her best china for the occasion. 'We're so glad that Mum has such good friends and neighbours,' he says.

It takes me a moment to understand he is talking about Annette. It is strange to hear someone refer to her as 'Mum'.

'Yes, it is a good, friendly community here,' I agree. 'Annette is a big part of it.'

'We want to visit often,' says Tony. 'Be around if she needs us. Although it is a long drive.'

'Annette is quite self-sufficient,' I say. 'But she is so glad to have you around.'

Candles are lit, the birthday song is sung, Annette cuts the cake. Joan photographs it all.

The two little great-granddaughters wheel in a small trolley, on which there is a brightly wrapped box with a large purple bow. 'Grandma, grandma!' they chant. 'Open our present!'

'Goodness! What can it be?' asks Annette, as the little girls drag her by outstretched hands to the box.

The girls cannot stand still for excitement: tapping their feet, begging her to hurry up, bouncing around the trolley. Annette prolongs their suspense, plays it out, slowly untying the ribbon, lifting a flap…and out pokes a little white head, two small ears, and currant eyes surrounded by fluff.

'It's a puppy! A puppy!' the girls shout.

Annette lifts out the little dog, sits with it squirming on her lap. The girls pat and caress the puppy, exclaim about his tiny, soft paws, his pink, panting tongue.

'What shall we call him?' asks Annette.

'Fluffy!'

'Snowdrop!'

'Tiny!'

'No…I think I have a different idea,' says Annette. 'I will call him Edelweiss.'

*

I saw it yesterday, low on my hedge. A sasanqua camellia flower, already opened, already blushing pink around the edges of modest petals, already blooming in its own little allotted space. The first camellia of autumn.

I picked it carefully, brought it in and placed it on a small crystal tray. Spilt the water on my table, as I knew I would, as I poured in a little from a glass, to keep the flower fresh. Left it displayed for my later inspiration.

For more than twenty-four hours, the camellia bloom sat in splendid isolation. The window has not let in enough wind to disturb the petals. The cat may have come for a sniff, a sip of water, but I didn't see her. The petals now look less robust, more delicate, as if about to fall – I know these flowers are always transient, always a message about fleeting time, about days that should never be wasted.

I have done my duty today. Have I done my duty to this flower? Shouldn't I have been here, capturing the blush of petal, the rich curve of green leaf, the unfurling of moments? Is there a better choice?

This afternoon, Joan and I helped Annette with a street stall for one of her charities. We sold homemade cakes, knitted tea cosies which went remarkably well, second-hand books and the last of Irene's orchids. Joan also had blank greeting cards, printed with her own photographs, to sell. They were popular. Tired out after the effort of packing away the leftover items and storing the trestle tables in the community hall, we stopped at the fish and chip shop for takeaway, drove back to my place and are eating it lazily in the living room. Missy hovers.

The autumn leaves journal cover I illustrated last year has arrived, printed on good-quality paper, one of the still print-based publications with which I am glad to be associated.

'Aren't you clever,' coos Annette as she sits on the sofa with a vinegar-soaked hot chip in her hand. 'I won't touch it until I've finished eating. Wouldn't like to stain it,' she says, thoughtfully.

Missy has no such qualms, walks over and sits on the journal. I shoo her away. She darts under Joan's chair, sniffs the air in case anyone is offering a titbit.

'I think Missy loves you more than me now,' I say, as the cat circles round and sits behind Annette's legs. 'That sardine trick was very canny of you.'

'Well, I may not have your painting talent, or your eye for photography, Joan,' Annette replies, 'but I am practical. There is a place for common sense.'

'You're a very wonderful friend to us,' I say, honestly. Annette has filled a void, become more of a friend to me than I ever thought possible.

'We are simpatico,' says Annette. 'Do you hear anything of Irene?'

'Not a word,' I reply.

'They say she still visits that man,' Joan confides. 'Will not divorce him.'

'I can't understand how an educated woman could be so taken in,' I say, shaking my head.

'Perhaps it's about having someone to care for,' Joan reflects. 'Someone who relies on you. Even if it is all just an illusion.'

'Like Missy here,' says Annette, in a moment of sagacity. 'And my Edelweiss. I don't think for a moment they need us more than we need them.'

'Quite right,' I laugh, and decide to test Annette's boundaries.

'It's nearly six,' I say. 'What about a glass of wine?'

'Well…just one glass,' she smiles, stroking Missy's ear. 'Before I go home to feed Edelweiss. It'll help me to sleep.'

*

The phone rings early next morning. I am still in bed, Missy curled at my feet. Too early – no one rings me this early.

It is Joan. 'Dreadful news,' she says. 'Annette is dead.'

'Dead? Annette? But how –'

'A heart attack in the night. She managed to press the auto-call, but by the time the ambulance came, she was gone.'

'Oh, Joan.' I am thinking of the wine I gave Annette last night. Surely it couldn't have?

'At least it was quick,' says Joan. 'No long period of suffering and pain. We have to think positive.'

'But she had only just found her son…'

'Yes. They DID find each other. And had some happy times. Her birthday party…did you see how she doted on those girls?'

'Yes. All right. I'm going to get up and shower. Shall I come over?'

'Would you like to? I wouldn't mind some company. It all seems too quiet here this morning. I'll make breakfast,' offers Joan.

'Just some toast and tea, Joan,' I say.

'And an egg? Boiled or poached?'

'No, just toast please.'

'Oh, by the way…I have Edelweiss here. Until Tony comes to fetch him.'

'Mind your pot plants!'

'He's already chewed up a cymbidium. I've isolated him in the kitchen.'

*

When I arrive at Joan's, fresh from my shower and wearing a cosy tracksuit, face free of make-up and hair still damp, she has a pot of tea ready in a cheerful knitted tea cosy, bread in the toaster ready to drop and eggs on the boil. As she lifts out the lightly boiled eggs, I change my mind, and accept one in a floral china eggcup. We sit and eat our runny eggs with soldiers.

'Nursery food,' says Joan. 'So comforting.'

'I can't remember the last time I had a boiled egg with dippers.'

'Larry didn't like eggs,' Joan says. 'And anyway, we gave them up almost completely when it was bad for cholesterol. Remember that? Now there's a whole set of different foods to avoid. And butter's good again. All that effort I put into finding different ways to cook, to save Larry's poor clogged arteries. Who would have thought?'

'Yes, I know. These were a good idea, Joan.'

'I often boil an egg now,' Joan says. 'For an easy meal. Protein. Haven't got the heart to cook properly.'

'A little fillet of fish is what I do,' I reply. 'Quick, and there's the skin to share with my Missy.'

'Tony asked me if I wanted to keep Edelweiss.'

'Such a silly name for a dog!' I blurt out.

Joan laughs. 'Yes! I'd have to rename him.'

We both look at the puppy, sound asleep in his basket by the back door.

'But I'm not going to keep him. It's not as if Annette had owned him for that long – he doesn't know us. He'll be much happier with those little girls.'

'Was it awful?' I ask. 'Talking to Tony on the phone?'

'Awful,' agrees Joan. 'But there's that sensible streak in him, like Annette. He'll be OK.'

'Another funeral,' I moan.

'Yes, there seem to have been so many this year. Of course, some of them were bogus,' complains Joan. 'All that wasted emotion!'

'You know how sorry I am,' I say. 'But Bob gave me no choice.'

'All in a good cause,' says Joan. 'I hope Ralph dies in gaol.'

'Irene will be very lonely.'

'Irene is ignoring her real friends,' says Joan emphatically. 'If she had any sense, she wouldn't put all her eggs in one basket.'

*

Annette's son Tony donates a gazebo to the nursing home in memory of her. Joan and I watch it being built, on our walks around the village. It is a decorative, six-sided timber structure, painted white. Generous enough in size to be useful: room for wheelchairs to be gathered around a table for afternoon tea. When it is finished, baskets of scarlet fuchsias are hung at the corners; the effect is quite charming. Annette would have approved.

A dedication ceremony is held. Tony and his family are here, many of Annette's friends and nearly all the nursing home residents. Tony says a few words and unveils a small brass plaque; the choir sings a medley from *The Sound of Music*; Reverend Wilkie offers a prayer of dedication.

Afterwards, I have a few words with Mrs Enderby, who has been wheeled out to enjoy the ceremony by a member of the nursing staff.

'I miss her, you know!' she says. 'Annette was always popping in. Always brought me a magazine, told me all the news.'

I nod. 'I miss her too.'

Mrs Enderby beckons me closer. I lean down so that I can hear her confidential whisper.

'You know, Annette got my watch back for me.'

'Your watch?' I look at the old lady's bare wrist, for a moment missing her meaning.

'My grandfather's watch, the one that was stolen. Annette found it in a pawn shop and bought it back. She wouldn't let me pay her for it…oh no. Wouldn't take a penny. I was so grateful.' Mrs Enderby's grey-blue eyes glitter. 'Annette was a jewel of a woman.'

I agree; I wheel Mrs Enderby over to the table where refreshments are being served, find her a cup of tea and a slice of fruit cake. I had forgotten all about Mrs Enderby's watch. But Annette hadn't – impatient with police procedures, she must have gone back to the jewellery shop alone, and paid that enormous sum to retrieve the antique watch for her friend. Pawn shop, indeed!

Joan is taking photographs. Mrs Enderby and I smile for the camera, and a group photo is organised. I ask Joan to take some closer shots of the gazebo and the flower baskets that I can use a reference photographs. I have been itching to paint those scarlet blooms ever since I first saw them: I will paint a watercolour as a gift for Mrs Enderby.

*

Missy is perched on the wide top of the wing-backed chair before the window: curtains are drawn for night-time, and the glow of a single lamp glosses the dense silkiness of her white coat, illuminates the pale blue irises of her almond eyes as she endows me with a confident, unblinking look, as only cats can.

She rolls into a more comfortable position and settles for the night, as I fall into a rhythm, typing words as one might practise scales up and down, melodic quadruple octaves travelling the keyboard in that hypnotic fashion that lulls the mind and opens the metaphysical heart.

The night is chilly, a mid-autumn night, quiet and full of repose. I cannot hear any possums or flying foxes outside; these soft night creatures may go about their business unnoticed. There is no traffic noise, no parties in the neighbours' backyards, no sirens on the distant highway. It is just me, the cat and the keyboard, keeping our date with our elusive friend, and hoping she will turn up.

It's not as easy as you would think to get the words on the page, even with conditions so near perfect as they are right now, in my cosy room. I have decided it is time to record my life. My memoir, if you like. To tell the story of my parents' tragedy: my recovery from their loss, my marriage. To make sense of the bizarre attempts on my life by Irene's husband: to try and understand how life twists and turns, changes and suddenly breaks off. If I go suddenly, like Annette, my story will be here for Susan and Mike, to answer the questions they have never had time to ask. There is no road map for my old age: my parents were taken from me when they were much younger than I am now. So many questions I never thought to ask them, situations I never understood. Time that was stolen, years that they missed. I try and write honestly, to present the truth as I have observed it. To render each situation with the correct tone and hue; not to brighten the shadows or transpose the melancholy melodies into happy lies.

On my table, a single spray of cut orchid flowers rests in a crystal vase. Many of the petals have browned – some have fallen to the polished table top, littering the space with their shrivelled shapes. Others, still deep magenta, remain proudly in place, toughing it out on pale green stems that arch though the air like extended grasshopper legs.

As I type, the sounds of *Weigenlied* keep me company. The little music box tinkles, revolves and the tempo slows, gradually but surely, as if the invisible fingers playing the notes have grown old and weary, ready for rest. When the motor is wound down, it will be time for sleep: when the lullaby is finished, my writing time will be over, and Mrs Rickaby will enter a final slumber, deep and dream-free.

9 781760 417093